The McBays

Bob Self

L☼HT SWITCH
P R E S S

Published by:
Light Switch Press
PO Box 272847
Fort Collins, CO 80527

Copyright © 2018
ISBN: 978-1-944255-87-9
Printed in the United States of America

CHAPTER ONE
PIG ALLEY

It was October 9th, 1848 and the McBays were sitting in Pig Alley, between the Red Spur Saloon and the B/R Funeral home. The B/R stood for Bill Ross. Bill had a few cows and his brand on his cows was the same B/R as the B/R on his funeral home.

Bill Ross was a true friend of the McBays, and he would not accept a dime for the funeral that just took place for Ma McBay. Bill Ross was also the person who named the small alley, Pig Alley, the same alley that the McBays sat in while hoping to see Shermon, McBay's first son.

The reason the small alley was named Pig Alley was because of an old man that used to bed his pigs down in the alley at night, and then head out of town at sunup, leaving only the smell of the pigs, long after the pigs were gone.

One morning the town found the old man and his pigs still in the alley after sunup. The old man had died in his sleep. A note was found in his hand leaving the pigs to the town. The town ate the pigs and kept the name, Pig Alley.

Lance, the second oldest held a black metal box, and Reminton, Ma's third oldest son, said to Wyatt, "I guess Ma confided in Shermon because he had no wife or young ones to care for?" Then Lance said, "It could be part of the reason Ma sent Shermon, plus I have my blacksmith shop, Reminton you have your gun store, and Wyatt you have your job at the saw mill. You might say Shermon kind of does know the land and how to fight Indians a might more than us, don't you agree?" Then Reminton's wife KaSandra said, "That's right. Shermon makes his living fighting Indians and guiding people from territory to territory." So then Abigail, Lances wife said, "Well it has been two days since Ma's funeral and I wish Shermon was here." Brandy, Wyatt's wife agreed with Abigail and added, "I'm sure Shermon is on his way, but I wonder what is taking him so long?" KaSandra said, "We are all wondering why Shermon has been gone for so long, and I just can't believe he missed Ma's funeral.

Wyatt asked, "Who has the wire that Shermon sent?" KaSandra said," I do Wyatt and it says I'm sorry for being gone so long. I will explain as soon as I get back." Abigail asked, "Did the wire say Shermon found the men that killed Max or anything about the land in Waco Texas?" KaSandra said, "No, only that he had some trouble and that he was on his way back and not to worry." Lance said, "Well, we all know if Shermon could have been here for Ma's funeral he would have. I just hope he's okay!"

They all agreed with Lance and KaSandra said, "Well, I think we need to see about some lunch and maybe we'll hear from Shermon soon. The sooner the better." Then a voice behind them said, "I'm sorry I did not make Ma's funeral. I did the best that I could." They all looked at the large man. He was 6' 4" and 245 lb. You could tell it was all muscle. They all thought he looked jawbone mean, but then he smiled. It was a real nice smile!

Shermon was dressed in full buckskins from his shirt, trousers, and his knee-high moccasins. He wore two 44 Colts in worn holsters, and a 12 inch Bowie knife with a stag handle in a rawhide sheave. He also had a small skinning knife in his right boot, and carried a 44 repeating rifle. He had a buckskin hat on his head, and tan rawhide gloves on his hands.

Shermon was smiling, but also looked a little bit sad when he said, "mom was only 54 but she sure lived a full life. Everyone knew her as Ma McBay." Lance said, "Shermon we know that you were trying to get back before Ma died, the same as Ma was trying to hold on until you did get back. But Ma told us all that she knew you would do what you needed to do, and that you would make it back as soon as you could."

Then all the questions started. Shermon said, "let's get out of this Pig alley and I will explain where I was for so long, but I think we need to get some lunch and open that black metal box that Lance is holding. First, I have to say I thought you all would be a little happier to see me?" Soon as Shermon had said it, they all came up to Shermon with handshakes and hugs. It was his three brothers, Lance, Remington, and Wyatt, plus his three brother's wives, Abigail, KaSandra, and Brandy.

Shermon said, they were all so, beautiful as he noticed the curves and shapes of his brothers wives. He could not help thinking of Cheyenne Decker, the woman he had helped in Waco as he looked at and held KaSandra, Remington's wife. He then let her go and said he would tell them more about Cheyenne later.

He shook hands with Logan, Lance and Abigail's son, and noticed how tall Logan was. Logan had a great grip at only 16 years old. He then hugged Katelyn, Remington and KaSandra's fourteen year old daughter. Shermon said, "Kaetlyn you are almost as pretty as your mom, Then Valerie, Wyatt and Brandy's daughter said, "Hey, what about me Uncle Shermon?" Shermon reached out and picked up Valerie and gave her a big hug then looked at Dakota and said, "Hey aren't you glad to see me code man?"

Dakota came over and shook Shermon's hand with force. Even at 12 years old Dakota was tall and very strong. Dakota said, "Uncle Shermon I am glad that you finally made it home." Shermon said, "Code man so am I. You don't mind me calling you code man do you?" And Dakota said, "Not as long as you don't mind me calling you Uncle Shermon," and they all laughed. As they were there, they noticed Rusty the six-year-old lab growling. Marshall Utal Wilson said, "Call off your dog. I need to talk to Shermon about him killing three men in the streets of Oklahoma."

Shermon said, "Yes I killed three men that had killed our uncle Max. It was a fair fight. The three Reams pull down on me and there were plenty of witnesses that seen the gun play who would testify that it was a fair fight or at least it was self-defense." Marshall Wilson said, "Shermon, I liked your Ma, she was a good woman. I think you need to ride out of town as soon as you can." Shermon asked "Are you going to run me out of town Marshall Wilson?"

Marshall Utal Wilson said, "Shermon I am sure there will be trouble for you and your family if you don't leave town soon." Shermon said, " Utal, me and my family will be leaving in a few days, so don't push me too hard. We have things to do so we can leave, and as far as trouble for me and my family, I can handle it, but harm had better not come to my family. I came back to get my family and take them to Waco, Texas."

Then the Marshall said, "Shermon, the sooner the better. I am truly sorry about your Ma. She was in every way a good Ma to everyone she knew." Shermon said, "Thank you Utal, and I am asking you to give me room so we can leave town without causing trouble for you or the town!"

CHAPTER 2
THE STORY OF THE SAWMILL

Shermon and the other ten McBay's walked down to the creek next to their old homestead where they had lived for so many years. The creek, as they called it, was like a small river at times and they had so many fond memories spent there.

Their Pa died at the age of fifty-four, and was ten years older than Ma. When he died, she was forty-four. They had been married thirty years. That meant that she was fourteen and Pa was twenty-four when they married. That wasn't an uncommon thing back then.

Pa was only fifteen when he started working at the saw mill, but he was as big and strong as any man working there. James Steadman was a very happy man when he decided at the age of fifteen to come work at the mill for him. He did the work of two men. He worked there for thirty-nine years. When Wyatt figured that if his dad could work there for thirty-nine years, and Ma's brother, Uncle Max could work there for ten years, he would surely be able to work for Mr. Steadman as well.

Max had a few small time jobs before going to work at the mill at age twenty-five. Mr. Steadman was looking for help at the mill and Max Cooper was without a job, so Ma told her brother Max that she thought he should go talk to James Steadman about a job. Max did, and was hired the same day!

Uncle Max worked at the saw mill for ten years, and at the age of thirty-five he quit. He said he had had enough of the saw mill and was going to prospect for gold.

Max's leaving was very hard on Ma and Max. You see, Ma was nine years older than Max when she married Pa. She was fourteen and Max was only five. So when Ma and Pa moved into the one bedroom house before it became a homestead, Max moved in with them. He stayed there until he decided to leave at the age of thirty-five.

Ma was only fourteen, but she was the only thing to a Ma that Max had ever known. Ma never knew her Pa and was only thirteen when her Ma had died from the fever and left Ma with her little brother at the age of four. So, when Ma married Pa a year later at the age of fourten, she took Max with her to the one bedroom house, and raised Max as if he was her son.

At the age of fifty-one, Ma was sent a wire from Oklahoma saying that her brother Max, only forty-two, had been shot and killed by three men who were after him for his gold. Funny thing though, Ma had previously received a wire from Max telling her that he had already turned the gold into land. He gave her the names of the three men chasing him, Tom, Johnny and Lonnie Reams, but that was almost three years ago.

Three years ago was when Ma had requested Shermon to find the three men that had killed her brother and to see to it that they got what was coming to them. She also wanted him to check out the land that Max had bought with the gold before getting killed by the Reams.

CHAPTER 3
THE BLACK BOX

After all the McBays got comfortable by the river side next to the old homestead, Lance handed the black box to Shermon. Lance said, "Shermon you probably know most of the contents that is in this box, so I want you to open it." Everyone agreed because he was the oldest. Shermon took the box and opened it. There was a map of a piece of land in Waco, Texas, and a paper stamped "legal note of the State's Courts of Texas." "There was a letter to my sister, who I loved very much, and to my only other relatives that I also loved very much," he said.

The letter said, "Sis, you are the best sister and closest thing to a mother that I've ever known. Sis, I left our home in Kansas City, Missouri to get rich—and I did! I hit a very large gold field, and I hit it big!" Max continued, "I have three men hunting me for the gold, but I don't have it anymore. I turned the gold into land and a future for my four nephews and their families. Here is the deed to the land and it is all legal. The deed is for ten square miles, 6,400 acres, ten mile by ten mile of the best land that money could buy. There's more land that joins this land if you ever want to purchase the extra land. You could even trade some of your water rights for the purchase of more land in the future.

The 6,400 acres has water rights for your land only and is the best horse country in Texas or   anywhere else! Before I say goodbye, I want to add, I hope you fellows understand why your Ma asked Shermon to slip away and go by himself? One reason that we, your Ma and me believe that Shermon is part of the land. He knows the Indians and bad men, and would survive to do the job at hand! Well, the Reams are closing in on me. They are maybe one day behind me, so I will see you all in the hereafter, Love, your uncle Max."

There was also another deed signed by the court of Waco, Texas, and attached, a bill of sale. There were names of people to see and pictures of land plots. The deed to the, now five bedroom homestead, was also included. That was where Ma lived and called her home up until the day that the good Lord had called her home to be with him in heaven. There was a note in the box asking them to sell the homestead to the caretakers for a price fair for all. Shermon said that Ma had received all these papers prior to the last wire that she received from the Marshall stating that Max Cooper had been shot to death.

The Marshall said it looked a little suspicious, like three men were following Max for a few days, when they caught up with him and killed him. He also said he was not sure if the three men took anything or not. All of his gear had been gone through and thrown about, but his horse, pack horse, and guns were still there when they found his body. So, that's when your Ma asked Shermon to investigate his murder. I told her I would look into it later when we had the time to do so. Ma had asked me to bring the three Reams to justice, and to locate the 6,400 acres in Waco, Texas. I told Ma, that I wouldn't have it any other way. I knew Max would do it for me.

So I grabbed my gear and had only three things on my mind, Tom Reams, Johnny Reams, and Lonnie Reams! Later on, I found out that there was another one, Zach Reams. He was said to be fast and mean but was out of the area at the time of Max's killing, so I wasn't looking for him. My whole idea was to see to it that the three Reams were brought to justice for the killing of Uncle Max!

CHAPTER 4
WHERE WAS SHERMON FOR ALMOST THREE YEARS?

Shermon said so I did what Ma wanted me to, to report on the land in Waco, but even more than that, she wanted the three Reams that killed her brother. She wanted them to get what they deserved. She could not believe that anyone would hunt a man down and kill him for what she called, "a little gold!"

Wyatt then asked, "But why did it take you three years Shermon?" Shermon replied, "Well, it's a long story, but I will tell you what I can now, and more later, if you all want me to? First, I let it be known that I was hunting the men that killed Max Cooper. That was easy. I was sitting on Buck, almost in the middle of town when the Reams came around to where I was sitting. They went for their guns. Well I guess they were slower than what they thought, and I was just faster.

After the smoke lifted, there were three dead Reams lying in the street. I also had an edge because there's not many horses like Buck that will sit still when there's gun play." Reminton asked, "What about Zach Reams? Don't you think he will want revenge for his dad and two brothers?" Shermon said, "Zach Reams is supposed to be mean and I'll cross that bridge later I'm sure. A couple of Zach's good buddies testified that I had gunned his family down in cold blood, but there were other cowboys on the street that day also who will testify that it was a fair fight. Anyway, I still wanted to see Waco, and get back to you with the news before Ma died."

So then Reminton asked," What happened with the more than two years you were gone and all Sherm?" Shermon said, "Well you might say that I lived with the Apache Indians for better than two years." Then Kasandra spoke up, "What do you mean you lived with the Apache Indians when we were all waiting for you to return?" Shermon said, " Hold on. You see it was not my idea. I was mostly trying to survive. I believe I must have been dozing off in the saddle and had no way of knowing the Indians were there. We were on a knoll and they were below us. Buck and me were on our way to Arkansas, riding high on the open plains when they came upon us. They were on all four sides of us before we knew it.

Like I said, I must have been cat napping and there was no way Buck could have smelled them being so much lower than where we were on that high knoll. By the time Buck did smell them and started snorting, I seen them and it was too late! They were on us and I just sat there waiting on them to take us, and they did. I knew if they did not kill me, I would escape the first chance I got."

Wyatt asked, "So it took you two years before you could escape?" Shermon said, "It took me three times to try to escape but I'm back now. So, do you want to hear about it now or later?" They all agreed they wanted to hear about it now.

CHAPTER 5
LIVING WITH, OR SURVIVING THE APACHE INDIANS

Shermon started by saying, "The Apaches are a very proud people and the reason they did not kill me is because they don't understand a brave white man. They did respect the bravery and the quality of being brave. Courage is one of the most important things an Indian brave can show his father and his father's people."

Reminton asked Shermon, "Why did you have so much trouble escaping?" Shermon said, "Well you see, the Chief of the Apache's is an Indian called Geronimo, and he is the smartest Indian I have ever met. You see, I did escape the very first week after being captured. I took off one morning before sunup, and two days later I was captured for the second time. The Indians tied me up by my feet, and all the young braves threw rocks, sticks and even dog turds at me. Then after all that, I got whipped with a bull whip by an Indian who really knew how to cut a person with a bull whip! I had no shirt or moccasins on, so when I was untied, I fell to the ground and then whipped with latigos. So for anyone who does not know what a latigo is, it's a wide piece of leather strapping used to clinch a saddle. Where I fell, I laid for three days and had very little water and no food. I also knew that if I did try again and got caught, it would even be worse than the first time.

My job was to carry fire wood and water to Geronimo's tent and then to other tents. I would get the firewood from a large wood pile and then get the water from a good sized stream. That's when I decided the stream would be a good way to escape.

I was watched very closely during the day, and tied up at night. This lasted over three months after my first attempt at trying to escape. I thought of not making it through the woods, so I decided that the stream would be the best way to escape. My biggest hope was that the stream would grow into a large river, the farther I got down stream. The stream was three to four feet wide and maybe two feet deep at the camp. I knew that I needed to go north and the stream ran to the north. I was sure that the stream was my best chance for escape, and I was sure that there would be more water to the north.

It was a long couple more months before my chance came to escape the second time. Hopefully this time I would make it. It was better than eight months since I was first captured and I knew that I had better plan my next escape real good. I knew if I tried again and got captured I most likely wouldn't get a third chance!

I knew that I would not be missed until morning when I should be adding fuel to the fires from the large wood pile. I figured that I would have at least eight hours head start if I planned the escape just right. I was hoping that would be enough time for me to get away.

I hit the stream at a dead run. The water was cold but felt good. It felt like freedom! I watched for real shallow water because I did not want to leave any foot prints in the creek bottom. There were times that the water pooled deeper and the stream even got wider, but I was hoping for a river.

The sun was up and I wished that I had gotten farther away from the Apaches camp. I was not sure how far from the camp I was. I knew I had walked, run, and swam, maybe at least two miles. I was praying that lead would hold, and keep me ahead of the Indians. I did not want to be caught again because I knew the beatings would be worse than the first time, and my guards would be doubled for a long time. Plus, I would be tied up at night with my feet barely touching the ground.

So, I started running through the water and praying I could stay ahead of the Indians until night came. I knew the Indians would not follow me at night because they believed that if they were killed at night, their spirit would never find them, and that they would wander the earth forever with no spirit.

It was not dark yet, but the sun was starting to set. I kept going as long as I could. My face was burning from all of the tree limbs scratching and bruising my face as I ran through the night. I decided to take a short nap, but when I woke up, the sun was already up and the fear of me stopping to long, and being recaptured, was also up! I had plenty of good water to drink, but very little food because I only took very little beef jerky and only two ears of corn that I had hidden the night before.

The food had been mine to eat at the camp but now the Indians would believe that the food was stolen and believe me the Indians did not take kindly to any kind of stealing. I ate the beef jerky and then the two ears of corn. I made sure to hide the corn cobs. I took a drink of water and started down the creek praying that I would not be recaptured. I was also glad that if I did get caught and recaptured, I would not have any food on me. You see, it would be even worse if I was caught with the food. I would get whippings for escaping again, but the worst whipping would be for stealing the food.

The first thing I noticed was that there were no sounds. Nature has sounds, good sounds that a person gets used to hearing. When I heard no nature sounds, I knew that was a real bad thing. The next sounds I heard were the sounds of being recaptured. It was only a few minutes later that I was being hogtied with latigos, which is the wide pieces of leather that I mentioned before.

You see, Indians don't use saddles, they only use blankets but they know how to use other parts of the saddles like no one else! When they tied you up in the latigos, and then they wet the latigos, the leather shrinks up real tight, plus dry or wet, leather strips make real mean whipping strips.

After having their fun of running me down with their horses, they drug me up and down the stream a dozen times or more. They had me tied by my feet so as they drug me, my head would have to go under the water again and again. Then one of the things I feared most happened. They brought out the two corn cobs they had found. The very ones I had hidden and hoped they wouldn't find. That was my second mistake, the first being captured again.

First, they tied the two corn cobs with the latigos and beat me with them. After they beat me with the corn cobs, they fed them to me by shoving them down my throat. I had open cuts and bruises from running through the branches and it made the beating even worse!

I guess I passed out because the next thing I knew, I was waking up back at camp, tied across an old Indian horses back. It was not over yet because that's when all the young braves had their fun. They threw rocks, sticks, and yes, even dog turds at me again.

The first person I saw was Geronimo and he was real happy to see me. I believe I had become his most prized capture. I could see a gleam in his eyes, as well as the Braves eyes. Then Geronimo turned and walked away with his three wives, the youngest one being only fourteen years old. The next one was maybe sixteen years old and the oldest one in her early twenties. Geronimo was in his thirties, but that's how the Indians did it.

The Indians hung me up by my waist with my feet barely touching the ground. All the young braves were either throwing rocks or dog turds, or hitting me with weeping willow limbs that really cut and hurt. Then I saw the bull whip. A large Indian brave was walking my way, smiling, carrying the whip. I was not happy to see that bull whip! The only thing that kept me going was thinking of my family. After being hit with that bull whip seven or eight times, I never felt anymore.

My mind was back with my family. We were making our plans for Waco, Texas. Then after the whipping I was cut down. I just laid there for a long time. Geronimo's son gave me some water and laid my shirt over my back. Soon I was back at my two jobs, carrying the fire wood and water. This time they added the job of feeding all the tribes dogs. I soon found out that I didn't like the dogs any more than they liked me. Once I got bit by a dog and it took forever to heal. I was also watched even closer than before, but I was already planning my next escape. I lost track of how many days it had been since my capture. I knew I had to stay alive and get back home, and at times, that's all that kept me going."

CHAPTER 6
THIRD ESCAPE THEN GETTING A FREE PASS

Shermon said, "I was learning their ways. I wrestled with the strongest Indians and I always won. I ran foot races with the braves and always kept up with them. I was slowly winning their confidence. They gave me a pony to ride, but I could only ride with the braves. My pony was much older and not near as fast as theirs, so they weren't worried about me running away while they were with me. Geronimo would not let me ride Buck, and Buck would not let them ride him. I hadn't seen Buck for a while but I still knew he was ok because they talked about him.

I was learning some of their words and now could understand them. I could even speak some Apache just as Geronimo could speak some of our words. I heard the braves saying that Geronimo was very unhappy with me for trying to escape again. I knew that when I did try to escape again, that I had to be sure to get away or it could be my last chance to every see my family again. I missed my family, my freedom, and even my black coffee. You see, the Indians did not drink coffee. They drank a tea made from herbs and berries. I never got used to drinking that tea.

I knew the right time would come for me to escape. It seemed like a lifetime, but finally I was leaving for the third and final time, hoping this time to be successful in escaping. The Indians moved their camp twice a year. One was their summer camp and the other their winter camp. Most all of the braves were up in the trees setting up their winter camp. The women were very busy getting their summer camp ready for winter. They set up summer camp in a large open valley and the winter camp where the trees would protect them from the cold and block heavy snows and wind. As they were changing their camps, I knew this would be the best time to slip away.

Geronimo's son had just left the camp to the south, so I grabbed a rifle and my old Indian pony and headed north. As I went over a small crest, I could see that my trail, and the son of Geronimo's trail was coming together. As I started to turn away I saw a Navajo Indian about to run his lance into Geronimo's son, whom they called Running Wolf. There were a couple more Navaho's trying to have their way with Geronimo's young wife.

I'll admit that my first thought was to keep going away, but I couldn't. I liked Running Wolf. He gave me water when no one else would, and Running Wolf was only maybe fourteen years old and the girl was not much older. It made me think of my young ones back home.

I knew the Navajos were renegades, and I wasn't sure how many more were around, but I felt I had to save Geronimo's young son and his wife, even if I couldn't escape. I was sure that I would get another chance, but maybe not as good as this one was. It didn't matter though because I had to save the two young Apache Indians. I knew I could save his life and he had been good to me. Running Wolf had given me water and food and even covered my back from the sun when I needed it the most.

Without thinking, I just headed my old pony right at the Navajos. When the Indian with the lance saw me charging him, he turned to throw the lance at me. I fired my gun and hit the Indian before the lance left his hand. The other Navajo reached out to grab the boy and I shot him clean off his horse! The Navajo's horse and Running Wolf's horse were both running away from the shooting. There were more Navajo's coming our way so I reached down and grabbed the boy as I turned the old pony towards the camp. There were two of us now on that old pony and the Navajos were gaining on us. I looked over and saw Geronimo's wife on running Wolf's horse also headed into the camp. There was help headed our way from the Apache's camp.

I turned the old pony again, just as a bullet hit me in the leg. The Navajos were closing in on us so I pulled on the reins as hard as I could and brought the old pony down on his side. I shot the Navajo who was closet to us and he went down hard, taking his horse with him. Running Wolf was behind me yelling to the Apache braves. I shot another Navaho as he was getting ready to put a war lance into Running Wolf. The Navajos were so engrossed with us, that by the time they saw thirty or more Apaches, it was too late to try to run away or escape. They had to fight but they were outnumbered.

After the Apaches gathered up the Navajos, they scalped them and left them without eyes so they could not find the happy hunting grounds or their spirits. When they got back to the camp, the braves told Geronimo what had happened and how I had kept the Navajos from killing Running Wolf and saved his young wife."

I was listening to the braves tell Geronimo how his son was saved from the Navajos. Even with Geronimo's strong face, Shermon could see the tears being held back as he was overwhelmed with the news. Geronimo embraced Shermon, and Shermon knew that Geronimo was sorry for the way they treated him, even though he would never say so. Geronimo did call Shermon his Great White Warrior of the Apaches.

Then the gifts came. Geronimo gave Shermon five large bowie knives, six beautiful beaded necklaces and two Indian dolls. The best gift was when Shermon saw an Indian brave walking towards him with Buck trailing behind. Buck had his saddle on and the brave had Shermon's 44 colts and long rifle. He handed them to Geronimo and he turned and handed it all to Shermon.

Geronimo said, "Shermon you are the bravest and strongest white man in all the land." Then Geronimo said, "My great while warrior, go in peace, and someday i hope to meet your family crossing our land to yours. But first, besides your horse, guns and your bowie knife, I want you to have this necklace."

Shermon showed his family the necklace that Geronimo had placed around his neck, and it was something to see! Geronimo said, "Shermon, all of the Apache nation will know that I have given you this and no harm will ever come to you. It is very strong medicine!" Then Geronimo said, "Go my Great White Warrior and bring your family through Apache Country with my blessings." Shermon said, "Well, I got up on Buck and we rode out and neither one of us looked back. I thanked God out loud. The only thing is, I guess I talked more than I thought I did."

Reminton asked, "What do you mean Sherm?" Shermon said, "It seemed like Geronimo knew a lot about our plans but I was still very lucky compared to others. I will tell you why later, if you want me to?" Hey," Shermon said, "Let's see what's in the saddle bags." Shermon took out four very large bowie knives and gave one to Lance, Reminton, Wyatt, and Logan, Lance's sixteen year old son.

Then Shermon looked at Dakota and Dakota was looking at the Bowie but didn't say anything. Shermon handed Dakota the bowie knife and said, "Dakota, I hope you like this Bowie." It was unreal. The ten inch blade was etched and the bone handle had blue like marble inlayed on both sides of the handle and also had a heavy leather sheath with rawhide tie downs.

Next Shermon pulled out five of the six beaded necklaces and handed one to Abigail, Kasandra, Brandy, Katelyn, and Valerie. He also gave Katelyn and Valerie each one of the Indian dolls that had been given to him by Geronimo, Chief of the Apaches.

They all thanked Sherman for the gifts and they told him they were not expecting anything but that they just wanted him to come back. Dakota then said, " Uncle Sherm, you know that blue is my favorite color don't you?" Shermon said, "That's right Dakota, I know that you like blue but I hope that it doesn't bother you that the bowie knife I gave you is smaller than the other four?"

Dakota said, "That's ok uncle Sherm, it's blue, it's sharp, and it's mine!" Then Shermon reached down in his moccasin and pulled out the knife that his dad had given him. Shermon said, "Dakota, my dad gave me this small knife when I was your age and I told your more than once that someday I was going to give it to you. Well today is that day! I thought that I may not ever be able to give it to you when I was captured by the Apaches, but I am giving it to you now!"

Dakota did not say anything at first but then he finally said, "Uncle Sherm I will always have it with me and if you ever need to borrow it, you can!" Dakota shook Shermon's hand and said, "Thanks!" Kasandra poured black coffee for Shermon and the other brothers. Kasandra said, "Shermon, you won't have to go without hot, black coffee ever again, as long as I am around to see to it."

Reminton spoke up and said, "Sherm, we all missed you while you were gone, and we all prayed every day for your safe return." Shermon said, "Well I'm glad to be back, and I think we should make plans for Waco." They all agreed.

CHAPTER 7
MAKING PLANS FOR WACO, TEXAS

Shermon said, "Well, if you folks want to go to Waco, we had better start our plans!" Wyatt asked, "Where should we start Sherm?" Shermon said, "Well, the first thing I think we should do is to see about selling the old homestead." Lance said, "Shermon, Ma wanted us to sell the homestead to the caretakers if at all possible. I know that Will and Jamie Casey, the caretakers, have already outlined the homestead. The five bedroom home, the large shop where my blacksmith shop was and Reminton's gun shop was on the other end. Then there was the separate sleeping area in between for overnight guests. Of course, first was listed the twenty acres with the water rights from the stream that we all had loved so much."

Reminton said, "Shermon I was told that the Casey's have already met with Jesse Dryer, the banker, with hopes of buying the homestead." Shermon said, "Well, we will check with the Casey's in a little while to see what kind of price they and Jesse Dryer have in mind. Then we can see if we all come to an agreement." Then Shermon asked Wyatt if he needed to see James Stedman, the owner of the mill, to let him know they would be leaving soon.

Wyatt said, "That was already taken care of." Shermon said, "Well, let's go see the Casey's and ask them what price they have in mind for the old homestead. Kasandra said, "While you men go see the Casey's, we will put a list together for the trail." Abigail asked, "Will you fellas be ready for lunch when you return?" Shermon said, "I know I will be ready!" Lance said, "Abigail that's a great idea, and I'm sure we will all be wanting something to eat when we return." Kasandra said, " Sherm, like I said earlier, I will make sure that there is plenty of black coffee here waiting for you when you men return!" Shermon said, "Thanks, Kasandra."

As the men headed over to see the Casey's, Reminton asked Shermon how long he figured it would take them to reach Waco. Shermon told him as long as they stayed on the trail they would be looking at 1450 miles or better.

Wyatt asked Sherm, "Why would we leave the trail?" Shermon said, "Indians, bad men, and weather will be a factor in the time it takes us to get to our land in Waco. If we travel six days a week and leave Sundays for rest and repair time, we will need to rest the animals as well as ourselves. We will also need the time to do repairs or grease wagon wheels and the like. I'm hoping we can make twenty miles a day. So, six days a week would be maybe twelve or thirteen weeks or around three months. If anything goes wrong, we will all pull together and shouldn't have too much trouble, although there is a good chance that every day will not be a picnic."

As soon as they walked up to the door of the homestead, Shermon said, "Let's plan on three months." As Shermon was saying it, Jamie Casey opened the door. Jamie hugged Shermon and the rest of the McBays that were with him. She said, "Do ya'll want to come in?" as her husband Will came to the door.

Dakota and Logon, said hi to Will and Jamie, then Dakota said that he and Logon was heading back to gather the things that they would need to take with them to Waco. Will shook Shermon's hand and said, "Shermon, I sure am glad to see you made it back!" He asked if he could do anything for him or the others. Shermon said, "Well, I hear you and Jamie are interested in buying the homestead?" Will said, "We sure are, if we can." Shermon said, "Our Ma wanted us to sell it to you and Jamie, and we know that you have talked with Jesse Dryer, the banker."

Will said that he and Jamie had talked to the banker and that with all the land and water rights, and buildings on the homestead, he thought $40,000.00 would be a good price for both parties, meaning the buyer and the seller.

Shermon asked, "Will, do you and Jamie have 40,000 that you can spend?" Will said that he and Jamie had $34,000, but that Jesse Dryer, the banker, would carry the note for the difference so they could by the homestead. Shermon said, "Let me talk with my brothers for a minute then we will let you know what we decide, ok?" Will said that he and Jamie would wait to hear from them.

Will and Jamie went inside and Jamie said, "I hope we can get this place for our own, Will!" Will said he also hoped they could, even if they started out broke. They could make a lot of money in different ways on the homestead. With the water rights and the sleeping quarters, plus, he always wanted to make wagon wheels and other large items, and the blacksmith shop would be the way of doing so. While the McBays were outside talking price, the Casey's were inside doing the same thing.

Shermon said, "Well, the Casey's have $34,000. What do you think about letting them have the entire place for $32,000? It might show them how much we appreciate all they did for Ma. With the other $2000, cash on hand, they can and will have a great start on their turn here."

Shermon's three brothers all agreed to the price after Shermon told them, he figured that $20,000 would buy wagons and oxen and all the supplies needed for their trip to Waco. Reminton asked Shermon, "Why oxen instead of big strong mules?" Shermon said, "Oxen drink a lot less water than mules, plus oxen will be a lot easier to control than mules and they are stronger. Let's go talk to the Casey's."

The four McBays stepped back onto the porch as Shermon stuck his head in the door and called to Will. Will and Jamie both came from the kitchen. Will asked Shermon if they agreed to the $40,000. Shermon said, "We talked it over and decided on $32,000 because of all the care and love you both gave to our Ma the last few years of her life." Will and Jamie were shocked at the price, but agreed to it when Shermon told them that he and his family would not sell it to them for a dollar more.

Will and Jamie both had tears in their eyes as they asked how soon they needed the money. Shermon said that they would be acquiring the wagons, oxen and horses in the morning. Will asked if he could meet them after nine in the morning, after he met with Jesse Dryer at the bank. They all shook hands and agreed to meet in the morning. Shermon said he could use some coffee and a biscuit. The other McBays said they could too.

After eating, Shermon said it was the best meal he had had in a long time. So, after some more black coffee, they thanked God for Shermon's safe return and asked God to help them now and on their journey to their new land.

They talked about things that they would need, and also about how long it would be before they could leave Kansas for their new land. Shermon told Abigal, Kasandra and Brandy the same as he had told his three brothers earlier, about the trail. He told of Indians, bad weather, and the chance of other bad things that could happen on the trail.

Then Shermon asked, "Well, do you think that we should get some shut eye, and start another day in the morning?" They all agreed to it and that night they dreamed of Waco, Texas!

CHAPTER 8
THINGS THEY WOULD NEED AND TAKE ON THE TRAIL

Shermon said that he figured they would need three covered wagons. He thought they should get the large Conestoga wagons with the floor size of 7'x12' and not the regular 4'x10'. They were called prairie schooners. The Conestoga could carry a much heavier weight if needed, plus there would be more room for people to bed down or sit inside if needed. The two front wheels are smaller than the back wheels so the wagons can turn much easier. Each wagon will come with a water barrel and a grease bucket to grease wheel hubs and wagon tongues as needed. Shermon thought they should have two ox per wagon so he figured they should need six oxen.

Wyatt asked Shermon, "Why not mules?" He said there were a lot of them around town at a real good price and not half as much as the oxen. Shermon said, "You are right Wyatt about mules being a lot less cost than the oxen, but a mule is like a dumb horse and maybe because a mule is half horse and half donkey! You see, mules are strong but not near as strong as oxen, plus mules can be very hard headed and nowhere as easy to handle as the oxen."

Dakota asked, "Uncle Sherm, you said a mule is half horse and half donkey? If so, how do you know which half is horse and which half is donkey?"

Shermon said, "Well Dakota, I will put it this way…When you breed a female donkey with a horse, you got a mule, and when you breed a female horse with a male donkey, you get a whinny and usually they are sterile. They are also normally very bull headed. The most important part of this is oxen are bulls that are five years old or more and they have been castrated which makes them very easy to control. Also, if we had to, we could eat one of the oxen. They are very good eating, unlike mules. I've known Indians that have eaten mules and even horses to keep from starving. Myself, I would rather eat an ox than a mule or horse.' They all agreed that they would rather eat the ox also, but hoped they would never have to make that choice.

Shermon and Lance met with Edward Smith, the owner of the six oxen, and Edward told them that the bank held a note on the oxen for $850.00.He thought the banker just wanted to unload the oxen. So Shermon and Lance went to see Jesse Dryer the banker. Jesse told him that he would take $900.00 for all six and it would take care of the cost of feeding and boarding them for the time he had them.

Shermon told the banker that he would be back in the morning to get the oxen. When Shermon and Lance got back to the blacksmith shop, Reminton and Wyatt were heading towards them. They had twelve quarter horses, all fifteen to fifteen and a half hands tall. Reminton opened the large doors to the blacksmith shop and they led the horses into separate stalls.

They had three, two tone brown one's, four black ones with very little brown on them, two grey ones with a little black on them, and three chestnut colored ones. Shermon said, "You fellows did good on the pick, how did you do on the price?" Reminton said, "Dusty Rodes said that the horses came from Montana.Reminton said Dusty told them that the horses were bred in the Bear Paw Mountains of Montana, and that these horses liked dry rocky mountains. as well as wet plains. He also said that these horses have the stamina and the well disposition to do whatever they were needed to do. Shermon then asked, "Ok, so what did we have to pay for the horses?"

Reminton said, "Well, with the twelve quarter horses they got four saddles and some leather goods for the total price of $2400.00."Shermon said, "That really sounds good but you didn't get any Latigo straps did you?" They laughed at that. Shermon then said, "Well, let's see if we can put a list together for the dry goods." Shermon looked around the large blacksmith shop and said, "I almost forgot how big this building was!"

Wyatt said, "Anything else would be too small next to that big five bedroom house. That large house is what I really don't understand." Shermon said, "Well Ma and Pa started out in a one bedroom house with Max sleeping under the porch roof. So first, Pa boxed in the porch for Max, which later became a large outside dining room. Then every time Ma got pregnant, Pa would add on another bedroom. After four new bedrooms, and the first bedroom, it made the house a very large five bedroom house with a large dining room. It was not a two bedroom house anymore, which started out as a one bedroom with a kitchen. Ma could have no more kids, but she would have if she would have been able to.

Pa was not done building. They had no need to build onto the house, so he started this large building and I'm sure he would have built another building if he hadn't died when he did. So, the large house, and this large building was Pa's idea to keep his family together on the twenty acres. It was just dirt and water when Pa started. Now we are selling it, and we will build our dreams in Waco."

CHAPTER 9
WHAT THE MCBAY'S WILL HAVE LEFT, AFTER THEIR PURCHASES

Shermon said, "Let's put a list together so we know what we've spent and what we have gotten for our money, plus what we have left." First they wrote down:

three Conestoga wagons with contents-$12,000.00

Six oxen with yolks-$900.00

Twelve quarter horses with four saddles and leather goods-$2400.00

Dry Goods split in three wagons—90 pounds of flour-120 pounds of white beans-90 pounds of rice-90 pounds of salted bacon-60 pounds of beef jerky-90 pounds of potatoes-15 pounds of green onions

30 pounds of pure salt and 15 pounds of coffee

Shermon said, "Let's get this list to Roger Miller at the general store so he can get a tally on it." So in the morning they had a good breakfast and checked with Roger Miller at the general store. Roger had the tally on the items and most of the items ready. The total of the items was $400.00

But then they added 10 pounds of sugar and two large tarps, plus a couple of other items which brought their total to $20 more. Now they were at the total of $15,720. They decided to buy a grave marker for their Ma and PA and then leave a few dollars for flowers in which they would leave with the caretakers, the Casey's.

The two markers of $20 each, and the $40 that they gave Will, and Jamie Casey for flowers, gave them a total now of $15,800 spent. That still left them $16,200 from the $32,000 they had received for the homestead. Shermon said, he thought they did real good on all of their purchases. Now they needed to split up the dry goods, guns, and ammo in the three wagons in case they might lose one of the wagons on the trail. If they did lose a wagon they would still have supplies in the other two.

Shermon said, "I hope we don't lose the wagon, but with Indians, bad men, and even bad weather, anything could happen. It's better to be safe than sorry, and better to lose part then all of our dry goods and guns." So they hooked The Oxen to the three wagons. Shermon said, "Let's split the guns."

In the first wagon, Shermon puts the 10 gauge side-by-side with the 10 gauge shells plus one 12 gauge and some shells and one of the 44 rifles with a few more shells. In the second wagon, Shermon put two 12 gauge side by sides and some shells plus 2- 22 rifles and some shells and 1-44 rifle and some shells and the Buffalo Gun with the shells. In the third wagon, Shermon put the last 12 gauge side-by-side and some shells, plus the last 22 rifle and shells and a 44 rifle with some shells. With the last rifles Shermon took his, Lance, Remington and Wyatt each took one and then KaSandra took hers. Shermon had his two 44 Colts and his extra one in his saddlebags. Lance, Remington, and Wyatt each, were wearing a colt and had one in their saddlebags. That left two Colts and KaSandra had them both. She said one was to wear and one extra if needed.

Shermon said, "Let's split the tools up in the last two wagons. Fill the two boxes on the last two wagons and if there's more tools, put those in the first wagons toolbox. He also said to put an extra water barrel in the last wagon and the other in the second wagon. We will fill them when we fill the other three barrels. Before leaving town, Shermon said, "Let's go see Rodger at the General Store. We will take three wagons and split the dry goods as we load the three wagons.

At the store, they put 30 pounds of flour in each wagon. They put 30 pounds of white beans in the first and the third wagon, and 60 pounds in the second wagon. They put 30 pounds of white rice in each of the three wagons. Then they put 30 pounds of smoked salted bacon in each wagon and also put 20 pounds of beef jerky in each wagon. Then they put 30 pounds of potatoes in the wagons plus 5 pounds of green onions in each wagon. Next, they put 10 pounds of salt and 5 pounds of coffee in each of the three wagons. Then they put 5 pounds of sugar in the first wagon 5 pounds in the second wagon, the large dining tarp in the second wagon, and the other two tarps in the third wagon.

. Shermon said, "We can hunt squirrels, rabbit, or deer as we go, plus we will fish and have duck eggs and anything else we feel fit to eat. There are lakes with catfish, and rivers with trout, and prairies with quail and pheasants plus who knows what else." They agreed to take their large Dutch oven to make biscuits and pies plus they also wanted to take their large dinner bell.

Shermon said, "Let's put them in the last wagon because I still think we need floor space in at least two of the wagons." He also said there were towns along the trail, "but believe me, we need to avoid them as much as possible. I think only two or three of us should ever leave the wagons at one time, and only when we have to, and the rest will need to be on their guard."

I don't mean to scare anyone, but like I said, there are plenty of bad men out there and would be looking for easy prey. We don't ever want to look like prey, or let our guard down to become easy prey."

CHAPTER 10
THE MCBAY'S ARE LOADED FOR WACO TEXAS

After a good breakfast, and plenty of black coffee the McBay's were ready to gather the rest of their items for the trail. Rusty was with them, and as ready as they were to get started. Rusty was about six years old, and he was a large yellow lab. Valerie with her mom and dad had Rusty since he was almost five weeks old. They fed Rusty with a bottle until he was old enough to eat. Most of the time, Valerie referred to Rusty as her big yellow dog, and Rusty was always by Valerie's side. So wherever Valerie went, Rusty went!

Valerie was five years old when they got Rusty from Will, and Jamie Casey, the caretakers of the homestead. A wolf had killed Rusty's mom and then Will Casey, killed the wolf. Rusty had two sisters in which the Casey's kept. They gave the boy dog to Valerie with Brandy's permission, and Valerie named him Rusty.

As they hooked up the six oxen to the three wagons, Shermon showed the women and the young ones how the yolk worked. The double yolk was a bar with two loops. They hooked two oxen to each wagon with a yoke and everything went smooth. Shermon said, "We will get our dry goods split up. We got our guns and ammo split up also. Let's fill our five water barrels and fasten each one to the wagons. We will put one extra water barrel in the last wagon and the other water barrel in the second wagon. Shermon said, "That sure is a lot of water, but it will be better to have it, and not need it, than to need it and not have it." They all agreed.

Shermon said, "We can always sell our wagons, and the oxen when we reach Waco if we decide to, and use the money towards our new place. So with that money and the money we have left from the homestead, we should do real good." He then said, "I think we should saddle five horses of the 12 and then we will have a remainder of seven horses that we can string out between the three wagons.

Shermon added, "I have six canteens here. I will have mine and one more on Buck, because I will be scouting ahead of the wagons. We will take the other five canteens and put one on each of the other five horses from the Remuda."

Shermon said, "We always want to have a canteen full of water on our horse. Other than guns, and ammo, split between the three wagons and us, plus our dry goods split between the three wagons, we can put the extra saddles and leather goods in the third wagon. We should always have our bed roll and a rain slicker tied to the back of our saddles."

We can put all our extra clothes and bedding between the first and second wagon, but leave as much floor as possible. If needed, we will have the floor space. Always have the horse blanket between your horsesback and saddle, because as far as a horse goes there's nothing that you could do worse."

Logan asked, "What is the main purpose of the horse blanket Uncle Shermon?" Shermon said, "You see, without a horse blanket between the saddle and the horse's back, the horse back would be rubbed raw and it would hurt the horse very badly."

He said, "If I repeat myself, it's only because of how important this is. I don't want to worry anyone, but we have to be ready if need be, okay? They all agreed and told Shermon that they understood why he was telling them. He had been there before. Okay, so you always carry a canteen full of water, your rifle with extra shells, some beef jerky, and maybe a biscuit or two whenever you're riding your horse to be on the safe side.

Shermon said, "Being prepared might just save your life. As they finish their lunch, Shermon said it is October 15th, 1848, and it is almost high noon. So if the wagons are all loaded with the tools mostly in the third wagon, and the dry goods, guns and ammo split between the three wagons, plus the extra clothes and bedding in the first two wagons, I believe we are just about ready to pull out and head for our new land."

Let's just make sure that we have everything loaded the way we want in the three wagons, then there will be plenty of floor space in the first and second wagon. They will be open for sleeping or sitting if needed. Whoever wants to can sleep under or next to the wagons, but not too close to the fire. You won't need the fire for heat, and you sure don't want to be a target sleeping in the light of the fire." Then Shermon said, "Well is everyone excited and ready to hit the trail to our new land?" KaSandra asked "Shermon, can we say a prayer before we head out?" Shermon said, "I think we should." KaSandra asked everyone to hold hands

CHAPTER 11
THE LORD'S PRAYER—THEN SHERMON YELLS—"LET'S ROLL"

So KaSandra started the prayer and they all joined in.

Our Father who art in heaven,
Hallowed be thy name, thy kingdom come, thy will be done,
on Earth as it is in heaven. Give us this day our daily bread,
and forgive us our trespasses as we forgive those who trespass against us,
and lead us not into temptation but Deliver Us from Evil
for thine is the kingdom and the power and the glory forever and ever
amen.

Shermon said, "Abigail you have the seat of the first wagon, Brandy you and Valerie with Rusty have the second wagon. KaSandra you and kaitelyn have the third wagon. Then he said, always have a long gun handy and pray that we don't have to use it." As they were pulling out Shermon said to KaSandra, "I see you have a Colt 44 on your side, do you know how to use it?" Reminton was next to the wagon, and said yes Shermon KaSandra is very good with a handgun, and also with a long gun. Shermon said, "That's good to know. Then Reminton added, "Abigail, and Brandy both are very good with a pistol plus a long gun, also Dakota and Logan has had a lot of practice with handguns and all long guns.

Shermon said, "Well I'm very glad to hear that we all have nine Shooters on this Wagon Train. Shermon continued, I will Scout up ahead, but I will never be over half of a mile ahead and I will be able to hear a gunshot. If you get into any kind of trouble fire three shots-- one right after the other, one, two, three shots. Never leave the wagons, but if possible put the three wagons in a triangle and take cover. Always show your guns, and try not to show fear otherwise don't stop unless you have to.

Shermon then said, "Lance, you, Reminton, Wyatt and the two boys, or young men, stay close to the three wagons. Flank the three wagons, one rider in front, two riders at the back, and one rider on each side at all times if possible. They all agreed to the plan. Then he added, keep your eyes and ears open and always watch the trail up front. Also watch the back and both sides of the trail. It is a good trail that we will be on. We always have to be ready for any trouble however.

Better safe than sorry, and the weather, well, I don't think we could ask for any better weather do you? I will find us a good place to make Camp, maybe ten to twelve miles ahead. This being our first day I don't think we need to go any farther than maybe ten or twelve miles." They all agreed to the weather being great and that they would stay together and put some miles behind them. So about ten miles later, they saw Shermon up ahead sitting on Buck his horse.

As they pulled up to where Shermon was, he asked, "Is everyone ready to make camp for tonight?" Reminton said, "Yes, I think that's a good idea because we are feeling our saddles and the women are feeling the wagon seats." Shermon said, "You all did real good for just the first day. There is a great area up here only about three hundred yards ahead of us."

So Shermon turned Buck and said, "Just follow me to our first night camp." They spotted Shermon off to the right and headed the small wagon train towards him. .There was a small knoll that Shermon said was there. "After we water the horses, we can picket them on the side of the knoll. There's plenty of grass for them and the oxen." So, after they watered the oxen, the oxen ate some grass and just layed down, content with the light wind blowing from the north.

They had the three wagons in a U shape with their animals between them and the knoll. They made a fire and put up their dinner tarp. There was plenty of dead wood around, so there would be plenty of fuel for their fire.

It wasn't very long before KaSandra was pouring coffee in tin cups and said, "We will have beans, potatoes, smoked bacon and biscuits with strong black coffee. Is that alright with everyone?" Shermon said, "I will have some beans and a couple of biscuits, but when KaSandra handed Shermon his plate, there was also a large potato and some smoked bacon with the beans and biscuit.

Shermon said, "Hey, are you trying to make me fat?" KaSandra said, "Now that you are with us there will be plenty to eat and hot black coffee always." Shermon said, "Ok, but I really don't need the large potato. I will try to eat the rest. After we eat, we will need a privy for a bathroom area, not too far away from the camp but just far enough. No one goes to the privy or even leaves camp without a guard!"

Brandy asked, "Sherm are you suspecting trouble this close to camp?" Shermon said, "I want you all to know we can never be too safe. Sometimes trouble comes when you least expect it. We can use those three small trees over there. It is far enough from the camp, but not too far. We can wrap one of the smaller tarps around the three trees and post a guard on the other side of the privy when it is in use. Like I always say…better be careful than not. Anything could happen. Indians, bad men or even animals can sneak up on you unexpectedly.

We will always post a night guard, and no one will leave the camp at night. The horses and Rusty will let us know if there might be something close to our camp, but a night guard can watch the weather as well as the wagons. Us men will be under the wagons sleeping or on night guard and you women can have the wagons, but I want you to keep a gun with you always.

Lance and Logan took first watch and when Reminton and Wyatt came to relieve them, they talked about the light streaks that they had seen from the East. Other than that, everything else seemed quiet while they were on watch, Reminton said to Wyatt, "You know I think we are really lucky to have

Shermon as our brother." Wyatt agreed with him and said, "Yes but I hope Shermon knows how we feel."

Reminton said, "You know Wyatt, I"m sure he does, but I don't see a problem with us telling him either. There's Shermon and Dakota at the fire now, Shermon is sitting on his heels pouring coffee, and Dakota is trying to do the same as Shermon." Then Shermon and Dakota walked up and Shermon asked, "Well are you two cowboys ready to get a couple more hours of shut-eye time?" Reminton and Wyatt both said they were.

As soon as Shermon and Dakota were alone, Dakota asked, "Uncle Sherm when do you think you will tell us more about your capture?" Shermon said, "Maybe Sunday on our down time." He then said, "We are on watch, so maybe we had better watch!" Dakota asked, "Uncle Sherm, what are we watching for?"

Shermon said, "First Dakota—we will never have this moment again. Yes we will have others, but we will never have this one again." He continued, "Code man we need to learn from yesterday, live for today, and hope for tomorrow. Dakota, always be yourself." Dakota said, "Uncle Sherm, a person could sure learn a lot from you, if they listen." Shermon said, "Well Dakota, I hope you listen to me because you know I love you. I want you and our whole family safe. Dakota you first listen to all the sounds around you and then say after half an hour, listen for sounds you didn't hear in the first half hour. Listen to the streams and other sounds, like birds or other animals. You listen to the wind and other sounds. Then you listen for any other sounds that you didn't hear earlier."

So they listened. Shermon listened anyway, because Dakota fell asleep. When morning came, Dakota looked around and said, "Real pretty morning isn't uncle Sherm?" Shermon said, "It sure is code man." Then Shermon said, "I am going to throw some water on my face, then I'll have some coffee."

Shermon walked down by the water's edge and pulled his buckskin shirt off. As he threw water on his face and hair, Brandy walked up with a tin cup of coffee. She saw all the whip marks on Shermon's back and could not believe her eyes. Brandy dropped the tin coffee cup and when she walked back into the camp, she was crying. Everyone asked why she was crying, but she could not answer them.

Shermon then walked into the camp and said, "Brandy, there's no coffee in this tin cup?" Through her tears, Brandy managed to ask Shermon, "I saw your back! How can you say you were lucky?" All the other McBays did not really want to see Shermon's whip marks, but they feared they had to.

Lance handed Shermon a tin cup with coffee in it and asked Shermon, "Is your back whipped as bad as Brandy is saying?" Shermon said, "Well, I thought I could keep from showing my back to you but I should have known I couldn't get away with it. I would have to show you sooner or later.

If you want to see my back, I will show it to you." Shermon pulled off his buckskin shirt and there was not a dry eye in the camp. There was way more whip marks than anyone could count. His whole back was covered, even his arms and neck. The family was speechless for some time.

Then Reminton said, "Sherm, if you were lucky, I'm sure we don't know how you can say you were lucky!" Shermon put his buckskin shirt back on and said, "Yes, I was lucky that I lived. I will tell you some of the awful things that I saw while I was captive. I knew I had to stay alive and return to my family. I'm sure that is how I survived my capture!" He continued, "I promise I will tell you the whole ugly story later but now I think we should have a biscuit and then break camp and make some miles.

Everyone hugged Shermon and told him how sorry they were about his whippings and how grateful they were that he did make it. They also told him how upset they were with what he had endured with the Indians. Shermon then said, "Remember what Ma would say? The heaviest thing a person could carry is a grudge. So maybe it was a miracle that I lived through this ordeal. Lately, I believe in miracles!"

As they ate, they all thought of Shermon's whipping, even as he was saying how good the meal was, and the coffee. Then he said, "Let's break camp and hook up the wagons and put some miles behind us.

Valerie was washing off Rusty at the stream with Wyatt on guard duty when they saw the camp being cleaned and the wagons being hooked up. Wyatt said, "Let's go Valerie before we get left behind." Reminton said, "Sherm I smothered the fire but I left the rocks for whoever might stop here next." Shermon said, "It's good to clean camp but it is also good to leave some dead wood and a place for the next people to build a fire. Let's take our places and I will be only a short distance ahead of you. Remember to flank the wagons on all four sides and stay ready for the unexpectable!"

Before Shermon pulled away, Valerie asked, "Uncle Sherm, my dad said if we didn't hurry from the creek, you would leave us behind, you wouldn't would you?" Shermon said, "Valerie your dad was probably saying that it is rude to keep people waiting, and that he is sure that people have been left behind before, but honey, believe me…I am not going to leave anyone behind on my watch and you can bet on that!"

CHAPTER 12
A SMALL BAND OF INDIANS LOOKING FOR A HANDOUT

Reminton was the first to notice a group of Indians heading toward them. Remington rode over to where Lance was, and Wyatt turned his horse toward his two brothers. He asked, "Do you think we should fire three shots for Shermon?" Reminton said, No, I don't think so, but have them pull the three wagons on. Make sure they have a long gun ready and make sure that the Indians see the guns. When they reach the small knoll, they should put the three wagons in a triangle. Like Sherman said try not to show fear and let him do the talking."

When they got to the small knoll they pulled the three wagons in a triangle and all took cover, but they showed their guns. As the Indians reach the small wagon train, they asked for food and why they had so many guns pointed at them. But before Reminton could answer, Shermon pulled up and told the Indians to move on. One Indian brave said, "We are hungry. Feed us and we will leave."

Shermon noticed that every member of his family did have a gun pointed at the Indians. The one brave held up his hand as in peace and Shermon did the same. Again the one brave asked why so many guns pointed at us? The other brave had his hand up and said, "We come in peace yet you have your guns pointed at us?"

Shermon said, "Our guns are pointed in your direction in case you decide that you have changed your mind about peace." The one brave said, "We have come in peace. We are hungry and we believe that you have plenty of food in those three wagons, and you have horses, and guns and food and we have none. We are poor and you are rich. We have no guns we have no horses and no food. Give us food, and give us guns and we will be your friends and not your enemies. This will be your choice big man."

Shermon then said, "We are all peaceful. We will fight if we have to. We will not give away our guns, but we will give food to your old and very young ones, just one time." The brave said, What about us braves?" Shermon said, "We will not give you or the other braves any food. You have bows and arrows. You can hunt if you are hungry." The one brave who was leading the small band of Indians then said, "If you don't give us food we take it!"

Shermon said, "If you try, then you will die." The brave looked around, and remembered all the guns pointed at him. "I will let you give food to our old and young and then we will hunt to feed ourselves." Shermon asked Brandy and Abigail to put some bread, and beans in a food sack, enough for the old and young ones.

Then Shermon told the brave to move his people on, and they could eat in the cover of the trees if they wanted. Again Shermon reminded the brave that this would be their only meal from the McBays.

KaSandra asked Shermon, why feed the old and the young and not the braves?" Shermon said, "The Young and the old could not hunt but the braves could and would if they were forced to. The main problem about feeding the braves now is if we feed them once, we would have to keep feeding them or kill them later. Also, we don't have enough food to feed all of the Indians that we might meet now and later on the trail. The small band of Indians, are sure to have other family and friends in the area, and they would demand a hand out also."

Shermon continued, While we are stopped, let's have a biscuit and some coffee and then we can make a few more miles before night camp." After lunch they cleaned up the area, and Shermon took the lead, and the rest of the McBays fell in where they were before stopping for the small band of Indians. Not only were they watching behind them, Rusty their big yellow lab was also.

Lance said to Reminton, "The weather is pretty good but it looks like rain is heading our way." Before Reminton could answer Lance a light rain had already started. The light rain felt good and even the animals seemed to enjoy it. Reminton said I hear shooting up ahead and then they all had to worry about Shermon a little. Then Reminton said I'm sure Shermon would fire three shots together if he needed to warn us. So Dakota said, What if it is Uncle Sherm, and he could use our help? I think maybe a couple of us should ride out and find him."

Wyatt said "Dakota remember Uncle Sherm said not to leave the wagon, train so let's just wait a little. I'm sure Sherm's okay. Let's watch for him and let's watch the trail."

Logan asked. "You think those Indians could have gotten ahead of us?" Lance said, "No, I seen those Indians making off to the east into those trees back there. That band of Indians didn't have any guns either." Then Shermon came riding up. Reminton pulled up ahead of the wagons and said to Shermon, "We heard shooting up ahead, and thought maybe it was you." "No", Shermon said, "There are some acorn trees up ahead and I believe there's a couple of guys squirrel hunting, but they're probably a mile ahead of us."

Lance asked, "Then you did not talk to them or really see them?" Shermon said, "That's right, but I know you would hear the shooting and might worry some. Dakota said, "We weren't worried. I told them that you would be okay Sherm." So Wyatt asked, "What do we do, keep on going on or stop for the night?" Shermon said, "Well if everybody's in for it, we could pull off to the right of the trail. That lake over there is called Horseshoe Lake, because it's horseshoe-shaped, and I believe there is some real nice catfish there that we can have for supper. If you want we could gather some deadwood, plus buffalo chips. There are plenty of Buffalo chips so we could even gather a few extra for the trails up ahead."

CHAPTER 13
THE MCBAYS CATCH CATFISH AT HORSESHOE LAKE

The lake was like a very large horseshoe and there was a stream running into one end and another stream running out of the lake at the other end. That's where they watered the horses, at the stream. Leaving the lake then, they led the ox down to drink. At Shermon's request they had put the three wagons in a u shape or a three-sided square; you know a square with one side missing. There was plenty of shade, but they still put up their dining tarp and attached it between the three wagons with the lower end toward the lake, which was the opening with no wagon.

They picketed the Ramuda of horses on some tall grass close to their wagons and the oxen to another spot close to their wagons. The oxen had already eaten and we're lying down. Buck, Shermon's horse, was untied, but would not run far. So, Wyatt, Logan, and Dakota took up their poles and took the worms that Lance had dug up and headed for the water. In no time they caught a couple of nice catfish.

Shermon said, "Lance we will stay alert but we will go on with our fish fry tonight and tomorrow we have a wagon wheel that's in bad need of grease, plus the ladies said something about washing some clothes. Tomorrow, I think we will let the animals rest. It will be Sunday, so in the morning I think I will take Dakota and Logan squirrel hunting. We will have catfish tonight and try not to worry. Down at the lake Wyatt said, "That is some nice catfish that we have caught, and more than enough for supper so let's leave some for someone else. Wyatt, Dakota, and Logan cleaned the fish with Reminton's help. They cut the fish into catfish nuggets then they threw all the remains of the fish in the stream that was leaving the lake.

Wyatt said, "There will be plenty of raccoon and other animals feeding on the remains tonight, but at the stream not in our camp. If we did not throw them in the water to drift downstream the flies and whatever bugs would be on us, besides the fish remains." Reminton said, "Well, let's take these nuggets to camp.

When they reached camp, the fire was ready and Abigail and Kasandra took the nuggets and rolled them in mustard seed and flour then dipped them into the hot grease that was ready. They made cornbread in the dutch oven. Reminton saw Shermon and Lance looking where the smoke of the other campfire was, and asked, "Shermon, do you think it's anything that we should worry about now or tonight?" Shermon said, "I don't think we need to worry but I will say it again, we need to be ready for anything, at any time." Shermon then added, "It could be a small band of Indians or it could be gold diggers."

"Gold diggers?? What do you mean?" asked Reminton. "There's no gold around here, is there Shermon?" Shermon said, "Well our horses and every-thing else in this camp would be considered the same as gold to renegades, whether it would be Indians or other bad men." Remington then asked, "How can we tell just looking at their campfire?" Shermon said, "Well if it was a hunting party we wouldn't see any smoke, and if it was a large tribe there would be many more fires and much more smoke!"

Then Dakota walked up and said, "There sure is a lot of squirrel in them trees over there. Shermon said, "There sure is Dakota, so in the morning we will shoot some for supper. Then KaSandra called out, "If anyone is hungry-- come and get it!"

Shermon said, "We had better not keep them waiting," and they headed over to eat. KaSandra said, "There are catfish nuggets, corn bread, thin sliced potatoes, and hot black coffee."

She continued, "When we are finished eating and this is all cleaned up, us women would like to go clean up a little." So after they ate, the three women and two girls, plus Reminton and Rusty, walked to the water's edge. Rusty never even got into the water. As much as Rusty liked the water, you could see he was uneasy about the smoke in the sky from the other camp.

When the women, Reminton, and Rusty, along with the two girls got back to Camp, the mess was all cleaned up and Shermon, Dakota, and Logan had their rifles and 22 shells ready for the morning squirrel hunt. Then Shermon walked over to the coffee pot where Reminton already was. Shermon sat on his heels and poured a cup of coffee then offered some to Remington. After Reminton filled his cup Shermon said, "I know that everyone is a little or more worried about the other campfire. I don't want any surprise visitors tonight."

Remington asked, "Do you think maybe we should check out the other Camp?" Shermon said, "I think maybe we should. I would sleep better tonight if I knew it was nothing, wouldn't you?" Reminton agreed that he would sleep better knowing that it was nothing worth worrying over. Shermon announced that he and Reminton was going to ride over to the other campsite and see who was in front of them, like maybe even waiting on them. Shermon said, "It will be getting dark soon, keep the fire going and stay on your guard. Keep a gun at hands reach. We won't be gone long. I want us all to be able to sleep tonight without worrying about who is ahead of us." KaSandra said, Shermon you and Reminton, be careful. We will all be all right until you two get back."

CHAPTER 14
SHERMON AND HIS FAMILY MEET WES MON-TANA AND HARRY AUSTIN ON THE TRAIL

Shermon looked at KaSandra and KaSandra had a Colt 44 strapped around her hips and was carrying a 44 rifle also. Shermon smiled at her and she smiled back. He could see a serious look on her face. Shermon said, "Keep the coffee hot. We will be back soon!" Then Shermon, and Reminton rode out. Reminton said, "Sherm don't worry. KaSandra can shoot as good as any man can, plus Abigail and Brandy can also hit what they aim at. Logan and Dakota is also good with a gun so there will be people with loaded guns and I know they will be ready for trouble.

Shermon said, "That's good but I hope they won't have any". Shermon and Reminton saw two men sitting at the campfire, and Shermon said hello as they rode into the camp. Both men stood up, and one reached a hand out to Shermon and said, "We were hoping that campfire behind us was you." They shook hands and Shermon asked, "Who are you two?" The first one said, "I am Wes Montana, and this youngster is Harry Austin. After they all shook hands, Shermon said, "Wes Montana? Do they also call you kid Montana? "

Wes Montana said, "That's right. You know how a name can attach itself to you, and I was pretty young when I first picked up a gun." Shermon said,

"Yep I do know, but I also heard that you have gunned a few men down that might have not been in a fair fight?" Montana said you know how the rumors fly? And I can guarantee every man I ever shot was in a fair fight.

The reason they started calling me kid Montana was because I was only fifteen when I shot my first three men."Reminton asked, "Why so young?" Wes Montana said, "Well, I was 13 when three yellow livered cowards shot and killed my Ma and Pa So after two years, I taught myself how to draw, aim, and fire, and I got pretty fast. I tracked those three yellow livered cowards down, and they drew iron on me. I left all three dead in the street. Just like you did with the Reams in Oklahoma."

Montana said, "Shermon, me and Harry here seen the gun play, but it was no play. I've never seen anyone shoot from a horse the way you did, and the horse not move." Shermon said, "Well Buck is real good about that, and I guess that gives me an edge." Montana said, "Maybe so. You are fast." Wes (kid) Montana started to say something else. Shermon said, Well I wasn't gunning for them but that's just the way it happened." Then Harry Austin added, "Well Shermon, all I know is they didn't have a chance." Harry started to say something else and Shermon stepped in. Shermon said, "Montana, I don't know why you and Austin are here, but I have family back a good mile from here and I need to get back to them. Why are you two here anyway?"

Montana said, "Well I know you remember Cheyenne. Cheyenne asked us to find you and your family and to let you know Zach Reams has some good for nothing drifters with him wanting to make a name for themselves". Shermon said, "Thanks for letting me know, but I need to get back to my family." Then Montana said, "Well Shermon, me and Harry are pretty good with a gun and we would like to help if you would let us, plus we are already here."

Shermon asked, "Why make this your fight?" Montana said, "Well Cheyenne likes you and we work for Cheyenne plus we're already here." Harry Austin asked, "What is the plan Shermon?"

Shermon said, "Well, I guess I will have to kill Zach Reams and any other man that is coming with him." Reminton said, "I guess there is no talking?" Shermon said, "No! It's like trying to put tooth paste back in the tube. It just can't be done! I'm sure Zach Reams has told everyone that I murdered his dad and two brothers, and promised them our horses and wagons, and anything else that his gunmen wanted to take if they came with him."

West Montana said, "Shermon let me and Harry here help you keep your family safe." Shermon said "Okay Wes. If you and Harry here are hungry, there is catfish & cornbread back at the camp. Harry Austin said that sounded good. I've had nothing but beef jerky and water for a few days now." Reminton said, 'Well I know there will be hot coffee also back at camp. Shermon said, 'Let's head back" and then said to Montana and Austin, "Be careful of what you say when we get to camp. There's no need to scare my family. I would like to keep them back from the gun play if at all possible."

On the way back to the small wagon train, Shermon ask Montana how far back he thought Zach Reems and his group was from them. Wes Montana said, "I'd say only one day. Shermon said, Then they are pretty close. Let me tell my family who we believe is coming our way." As they got close to camp Shermon said hello in the camp. "Me and Reminton brought a couple of hungry cowboys with us." All Montana and Austin seen at first was a large fire. Then there were seven people holding rifles on them from different areas. Montana said, "Hey we are here to help don't shoot us!" Austin said, "Yeah we are friends. Shermon said, "It's okay. They were sent here by Cheyenne, a girl I met while in Waco." KaSandra said a girl? I want to hear about the girl Shermon!"

Lance then asked, "Help with what Sherm?" Shermon said, "Let them get something to eat then I will explain." Montana said, "I am Wes Montana and this gent is Harry Austin. We sure would like some of that catfish we've been hearing about." Harry said, "How about some of that coffee also?" They all shook hands and then supper was on for Montana and Austin.

There was catfish, cornbread plus there was some thin fried potatoes in which KaSandra called potato skins, and of course—hot coffee! Shermon waited until Montana and Austin were almost finished eating and as he poured them and himself a cup of coffee, Shermon said, "These two cowboys brought me some important news."

KaSandra said, "They said a girl named Cheyenne? How did you meet her?" Shermon said, "That's right Cheyenne, I will tell you all about Cheyenne but first I need to say that we might have a few unwanted visitors by morning." Wyatt asked, "What kind of visitors Sherm? Bad visitors you say?" Shermon said, "I'm afraid they will be bad."

Reminton said, "Sherm, I think we should tell them that it's Zach Reams and some others and that they are gunning for you!" Wyatt said, Zach Reams? Isn't he the bad brother that you mentioned earlier?"

Shermon said, "That's right!" Lance then said, "Sherm, how do we play this?" Shermon said, "I would like you all to stay in camp with your guns ready, and Montana and Austin will ride out with me to meet Reams and his drifters! We will try to end it away from camp, but if one or more makes it here, don't ask questions, kill them!"

Lanced asked, "When do you think they will be here?" Shermon said, "They will probably make it here tonight, but I don't think they will come into camp tonight. Just stay away from the fire and we will double the guard tonight."

Wes Montana said, "Shermon, me and Harry here will stand guard with you, if you like." Shermon said, "That would be good." Shermon continued, "Lance, you and Wyatt take the first watch with Harry, then Montana. Reminton and me will relieve you three. Don't become a target by the fire and if any of you see anyone, wake me!"

So Lance, Wyatt and Harry Austin stood watch, then Shermon and Reminton and Wes Montana relieved them. Shermon told them to get some shut eye and he would see them in the morning. Shermon walked over to the fire when the sun was just coming up. Reminton asked, "How do you want to play this?" Shermon said, "Like I said, I want you to stay back and I will go out to meet Zach Reams." Shermon continued, "I know you are very good with a gun and you want to stand with me against Zach Reams and his gunslingers, but I need to know that you will be protecting our family at camp if I should go down. Other than me, you are the only one in our family that has stood in front of a gun when it is firing back.

I know the rest of our family is good with guns because of you teaching them how to shoot." Reminton said, "I will do like you asked." Shermon then said, "I hope that Zach Reams drifters will back off when I give them the chance to live. That is why me, Montana and Harry Austin will meet them away from camp. I will be on Buck, and Buck and me have done this many times, where I shoot from his back and he will stand still unlike any other horse in this situation. So, maybe it will be the edge I need."

Wes Montana spoke up, "Shermon, me and Harry here are pretty good with a gun. We have been in our share of fights. We want to help, we told Cheyenne we would." Shermon said, "It's not really your fight." Montana said, "Shermon there is no way you can beat them all, but with me and Harry helping, the three of us might be able to win. So, we want to make it our fight."

Shermon said, "Ok Wes, you and Harry can ride out with me. He continued, "Kid, I won't forget this. When we get to Waco, look me up and there will be a job for you if you want it."

Shermon told Lance, Reminton and Wyatt to make sure everyone had a gun and to stay under cover, and if anyone but him, Montana or Austin came into camp, don't ask questions, but to shoot to kill. Shermon knew that kid Montana and Austin would take that shot and not want to be shot at first, but Shermon worried about his family being shot at.

When they were waiting for the sun to come up, Montana said, "Shermon, about that job...say if I would pull up stakes and come to work for you, what about Harry? Me and Harry have been riding together down the same path for some time." Shermon said, "When we get out of this mess, and when the time comes, there will be a job for you, Harry and a few more like you two."

Then Shermon asked, This Zach Reams, you know him?" Wes Montana said, "Yes I know him. He is mean and ugly and has a hell of a scar on his face!" Shermon said, "Can you tell me anything about him, anything that might help when I meet him face to face?"

Montana said, "I have studied him a little because I figured me and him would be standing face to face one day pulling iron. He's fast Shermon, like you, but he normally misses with his first shot. He wears two guns like you and he pulls them both. I have noticed that he blinks and raises his eyebrows right before he pulls iron." Shermon said, "Thanks kid. Knowing that and shooting from my horse should give me all the advantage I need."

CHAPTER 15
THE GUN FIGHT

The sun was up and so was Zach Reams. He had seven other riders with him. Shermon said to Montana, "Do you know any of the seven with Reams?" Wes Montana said, "No but I think only Zach Reams and two others are gun fighters. The other five are drifters and want to be's!"

Shermon was hoping to keep all eight of the eight men in front of him and away from his family. But, as Shermon, Wes and Harry rode toward Reams and the other seven riders, about sixty yards out, four of the riders split off, two to the left and two to the right.

Shermon was not aware that Lance and Wyatt had left the camp and was moving up behind them, one on each side. There were four men sitting on their horses in front of Shermon, Wes Montana, and Harry Austin. Shermon said, "Kid, you take the one on the left in front of you, and Harry, you take the one on the right, in front of you, and I will take Reams and the big one next to Reams". He continued, "Don't forget the other four that will flank us or try to head for my family."

Harry said, "Are we going to wing them, or kill them?" Shermon said, "We will leave them for dead if they draw on us. I don't want to lay awake at night because I didn't finish the job at hand today." They pulled up in front of Reams and the other three. Shermon said, "Do we kill all four of you or do you three others want to ride out?"

Zach Reams said, "McBay, you killed my Pa and my two brothers!" Shermon said, "I didn't want to but they pushed me just like you are doing now. Zach Reams blinked and raised his eyebrows but it was too late when he went for his guns because Shermon had already put two bullets in Reams and Reams fell off his horse and was dead before hitting the ground.

Shermon felt his ear burn as he fired bullets into the big man that had been sitting on his horse next to Reams. Harry Austin shot his man two times and both times in his heart. Wes Montana had shot his man threw the heart and also put a bullet into the big man that Shermon had shot twice. There was no time to delay because the other four men were gone and there was shooting back at the McBay camp!

Shermon yelled to Montana and Austin, "My family is under fire!" Shermon, Wes Montana and Harry Austin all raced back to the small wagon train and Shermon's family. Shermon knew the other four riders that were with Zach Reams were shooting it out with his family.

Lance had shot one of the riders, but Lance also had blood on his shirt that Shermon noticed as Lance fell to the ground. Shermon seen Wyatt and yelled to him, "Wyatt help Lance, he's been shot!" Shermon then headed for camp and Wes Montana was with him. Harry Austin stayed with Wyatt and helped him put Lance on his horse. Lance was bleeding bad.

As Shermon and Wes Montana came into camp the first thing they seen was Reminton with one dead rider in front of him and another rider coming up from behind him. Neither Shermon nor Montana could get a shot at the other rider with Reminton between them and the rider. Just then the rider was blown out of his saddle. It was KaSandra. Her 44 colt was in its holster, but she had her 44 rifle to her shoulder and said, "I got that gunslinger!" Shermon said, "You sure did KaSandra!"

Then Shermon said, "There was one more rider. We got four, Lance got one, Reminton got one and KaSandra got one. That's only seven. Then Dakota said, "Uncle Sherm, me and Logan got the other one. He was trying to sneak up on us and we both shot him at the same time. Rusty started growling, and me and Logan both jumped up and shot, then we took his gun."

Shermon said, "Way to go boys!" Then Wyatt and Harry Austin came in with Lance. Abigail and Logan ran over to him. They helped Lance off the horse. Lance did not look good. He had lost a lot of blood but luckily the bullet had gone straight through. Abigail cleaned the wound and put a nice dressing over it. Lance said, "I'm ok, but you need to check Shermon."

Shermon said, "Why me?" He had forgotten about the burning he felt during the gunfight. Wyatt said, "Sherm, you have blood down your face and all over your buckskin shirt. He said, "Yeah I forgot I did feel a little burning on my ear during the shootout." So Abigail said, "Let me wash off the blood, and then she said, Shermon, part of your ear is gone!"

Shermon said, "Here, take my knife and cut off part of my other ear so they match." Abigail said, "I will not, you have to be kidding!" Shermon said, "Yes, I am kidding" and he laughed. He said, "I think we were very lucky. I don't think we would have been so lucky if it weren't for you kid and Harry here." "My family and me are very grateful to you both." Shermon said. "I can't thank you two enough!"

Wes Montana said that him and Harry was glad to help and said, "Shermon, I think that you and your family would have been ok, but I am glad you still let us help." Then Harry Austin said, "Yea Shermon, if we ever go to war, I sure want your family on my side." Then Wes said him and Harry needed to hit the trail, and that they would watch for them when they got to Waco.

Shermon said, "Well, let us send some coffee and beef jerky with you and make sure you look us up on our new homestead. Wes Montana said they would and that they would stop up ahead at the next town and wire Cheyenne.

Shermon said, "Remember you two have a job in Waco with us once we get set up, and Harry you mentioned your son Mario? He will also have a job with us if he wants one. He continued, "You two be real careful on the way home because this family of mine won't be there to cover your backside."

Then Harry Austin asked, "What about that big yellow dog? If you want, I could take him off your hands?" Then all the McBays answered at about the same time, No way, he will be staying with us. Harry laughed and said, "See you in Waco." Shermon told him it would be about two months before they would make Waco. He said, "If you guys did not have to get back, you could travel with us."They all shook hands and Wes Montana and Harry Austin rode out.

KaSandra asked Shermon, "Do you think it will be two months before we get to Waco?" Shermon said, "Well, we just made Arkansas and we have been on the trail for five weeks. So, I would say it will be right at two months more."

Then Shermon asked Lance, "How do you feel brother?" Lance said he was fine and asked Shermon how he felt. Shermon said, "I could not be any better as long as everyone else is good!" Dakota said that he sure liked Montana and Austin but wondered why Shermon called Wes Montana Kid? Shermon said, "Well the story is that three bad men killed Montana's Ma and Pa when Wes Montana was just thirteen years of age. Wes Montana hunted the three men down and killed all three in a gun fight at the age of fifteen.

Dakota said, "At just fifteen, he killed three men! Wow, that's something!" Shermon said, "Dakota that can be a tough reputation to have." Logan asked, "What do you mean Uncle Sherm?" "See when you get a reputation as a gun hand or a gun fighter, there is always someone who wants to find out if he is faster than you are," Shermon said.

Dakota asked, "Don't you have a reputation Uncle Sherm?" Shermon was not sure how to answer, so he just said, "Half of the morning is almost over, didn't you two want to shoot some squirrels?" As they were reaching for their 22 rifles, KaSandra asked, "Who is Cheyenne and how did you meet her?"

Shermon said, "How about I tell you about Cheyenne Decker after we get some squirrels for supper?" KaSandra said, "Ok Sherm, but it seems like you have a lot of secrets." Shermon said, "No, I don't have any secrets KaSandra, there is only things that I have not mentioned as of yet. We have a long trail ahead of us yet, so I will tell you everything as we continue on our way to Waco. Dakota, Logan and myself, are going to walk over to those trees and shoot some squirrels. I don't think it will take us very long. Stay on your guard and get ready to have some nice squirrels for our meal.

CHAPTER 16
THEY FINALLY GO SQUIRREL HUNTING

As Shermon, Dakota, and Logan walked to the large oak trees, Shermon said, "It shouldn't take us very long to get the squirrels we need. All you need to do is be quiet and watch for the squirrels to move." As they walk toward the trees, Shermon noticed that Dakota had the skinning knife on his side that he had given him. Shermon said "Look, there's acorn shells everywhere here and I can hear them squirrels barking at us. Why don't we just sit under these three oak trees?" He then said, "Let's just shoot up into the trees because we wouldn't want to hit anything that we wouldn't be shooting at." In less than an hour they already had eight squirrels.

Shermon said, "Eight squirrels, that's good. Let's leave some for the next hunter's. Let's skin these squirrels and get back to camp." Shermon showed Dakota, and Logan how to clean the squirrels. Shermon cleaned the first two squirrels and then let Dakota and Logan clean the next six squirrels. Shermon and the two boys, or young men, walked back into camp. Dakota said, "We got eight squirrels! Me and Logan each shot three and Uncle Sherm only shot two." Shermon smiled and said, "That's right!" Shermon went to the fire and reached for the coffee pot when KaSandra grabbed it and said, "Shermon, we want to know about Cheyenne. How did you meet her?"

Shermon said, "KaSandra how about handing me the coffee pot and I will tell you about Cheyenne after supper." So KaSandra poured Shermon a cup of coffee and said, "I guess we can wait a little longer sherm." They cut up the squirrels, floured them and set them into the grease one piece at a time. They cut small potatoes into thin slices and added onions, and fried the potatoes and made more black coffee and biscuits in the Dutch oven. When they were done eating, Sherman said, "Boy that was a meal to remember!"

KaSandra said, "We are waiting Shermon?" Shermon said, "What are we waiting for?" KaSandra said, "You know Shermon, we want to hear about Cheyenne." Shermon said, "Well when I first seen her, I said to myself now that's my kind of girl." Shermon said, "Other than Cheyenne being so pretty, Cheyenne and me could have been twins because we were both wearing about the same outfit." Brandy asked, "What was Cheyenne wearing Sherm?" Shermon said, "She was wearing buckskin pants, a buckskin shirt, and moccasins, knee-high, and she had a Colt 44 in a holster on her hip, and a large bowie knife on her other hip."

Abigail said, "Well how did you meet this Cheyenne woman?" He replied, "There was two cowboys on the boardwalk in front of Cheyenne, and one was trying to get a kiss from Cheyenne I believe. KaSandra asked, "So what did you do to scare him?" "Well I walked right up on them two cowboys and I had a wagon wheel spoke in my hand. I guess the spoke had a mind of its own. The Wagon Wheel spoke hit one of the cowboys in the face and broke the cowboys jaw and then the spoke jabbed the second cowboy in the stomach and then across his face breaking the cowboys nose. All I said was I won't tolerate rude people, and I won't cotton to it! That's when I found out her name was Cheyenne, Cheyenne Decker."

Cheyenne first said to me, "Hey big man, I had it under control." I told Cheyenne that I didn't mean to but in but as I told those two cowboys I won't tolerate rude people. Cheyenne then said, "Well you sure swing a mean wagon wheel spoke big man." I wasn't sure what to say next. Cheyenne said, "Well let me buy you lunch and I will forgive you for butting in."

During lunch I told Cheyenne about Uncle Max being killed and about my gun fight in Oklahoma with three men that killed Max. Cheyenne said for me to be real careful because Zack Reams had a mean streak in him a mile long and she was sure that he would come gunning for me, and that he would not come alone. So that's when Cheyenne later heard Zack Reams was heading out of town and coming our way but he was gathering drifters and maybe a couple of gunslingers to meet us on the trail. Cheyenne ask kid or Wes Montana, and Harry Austin to find us first and just stand with me when the gun play started.

Shermon said, "Lance I'm sorry that you got shot, and I think you should take it easy for a few days. Give that shoulder a chance to heal." Lance said "Well Sherm, like you said, the bullet went through and I'm sure I can carry my own weight." Shermon said, "And I'm sure you can, but let's give it a few days and make sure infection does not set in." Lance said, "Okay I will take a wagon seat for no more than a few days, but then I want my horse back. It's going to be dark soon, so let's build that fire up and get some shut-eye."

Then Shermon said, "Wyatt, if you want to take the first watch and Remington, you relieve Wyatt, then I will relieve you a couple of hours later. I want you all to know how proud I am of everyone. I think we should thank God and Cheyenne for sending Wes Montana and Harry Austin to help us. KaSandra said, 'I already thanked God, and I will thank Cheyenne when I get to meet her."

CHAPTER 17
LEAVING THE TRAIL BECAUSE OF CLINCH BUGS

After quoting a few of Ma's sayings, Shermon said, "Well this Horse-shoe Lake area is pretty, but not as pretty as where we are heading." Remington then said, "Well, let's break camp and put some more miles behind us." They watered the animals, and tied eight horses to the wagons. After putting saddles on four of the quarter horses and the one on Buck, they hooked up the oxen.

They made sure all the water barrels were full and picked up camp. Lance rode on the first wagon seat with Abigail, and KaSandra with Kaetlyn was sitting on the second wagon seat. Brandy and Valerie had the third wagon seat with Rusty between them, and Rusty looked like he was happy to be leaving Horseshoe Lake, and getting back on the trail. Shermon checked his two canteens and his saddlebags, and took the lead. After throwing water on the campfire, as he pulled away he said, looks like God has given us another beautiful day. Stay alert and together, and I won't be too far ahead.

The weather was really nice with a slight breeze and no rain in sight to be seen. They were making good time but then they noticed the grass was dry, even dead. It was burnt looking. Even the leaves on the trees were dry and burnt looking. They were all studying the grass and trees when they saw Shermon heading towards them. Shermon pulled up and Reminton asked

Shermon what he thought had happened to the grass and trees. Shermon said, "It is clinch bugs. Reminton said, "Clinch bugs? I've heard of them but never seen any." Shermon said, "I have and believe me you don't want to be where they are." He continued, "It is swarms, which there would be very large numbers of clinch bugs. The sky would be covered with them, and the noise would be unbelievably loud. They are small white winged black bugs, and they suck all the juices and moisture out of everything. They kill the grass and leaves, where there is nothing left for horses, cows or any other animal to eat. I followed them up the trail for over a mile and it only gets worse. I hate to, but I think we should leave the trail, and return when we can. Let's cut off the trail here and we can catch the trail up ahead where the grass is good again."

Remington asked Shermon if he wanted him to ride up front with him and Shermon said he could help him watch the rough Terrain. Shermon said, "Let's ride at least ten feet apart so we can scout this terrain real close. I'm really worried about this uneven ground, and all these large hidden rocks right under the surface. Also, the short trees or bushes with these heavy barbs are really bad. Not only are these rough on us, they are cutting our horse's hide and it does not look any better for a while."

Shermon was just saying to Reminton that maybe they should have taken their chances on the trail, when he saw a clearing up ahead. Reminton broke through the short trees and bushes as did Shermon,. Then the rest of the family came there and reached the clearing with a sigh of relief. In the clearing Shermon said, "Let's pull over here and doctor some of these cuts and scrapes on us and the horses."

They were so engrossed with all the cuts and scrapes, that they did not see the trail up a head until they started moving again. Shermon said, "Well the grass really looks good and the best thing is there is no clinch bugs. Reminton said, "Looks like the clinch bugs went to the east and we are heading south. Shermon said, "I will head up and scout for a good night camp. I won't be too far ahead." After a couple of miles, they seen Shermon sitting on Buck and Shermon waved them to the left. As they turned toward the left, Shermon road up to them and said, "There is a real good site about 200 yards up ahead with good grass and a clover mixture, plus a very large stream with movement in the water, and I'm sure it is fish."

Dakota asked, "Do you want us to catch some for supper?" KaSandra said fried fish sounded real good. Brandy agreed with her the same as the rest did. Valerie said, "Me and Kaetlyn want to fish." Shermon said, "Anyone that wants to fish can, but remember that water is moving pretty fast and I'm not sure how deep it is, so we have to be very careful at the water's edge.

Shermon said, "I believe it is trout, so the fishing will be a little different than cat fishing. Dakota and Logan both said, "If there is fish there, we can catch them. Lance said, "I feel pretty good so I will help get some poles ready. Wyatt asked what kind of bait would be the best for trout?" Reminton said, "I think some corn would be the best don't you Sherm?" Shermon said, "That and real small worms on real small hooks."

The two boys, and two girls plus Rusty was already headed to the water when Reminton said, "Hold on a minute, Lance and me will be standing guard plus like Uncle Shermon said, the water is moving pretty fast so be careful." Wyatt was stacking rocks for their fire and helping put up the dinner tarp. Shermon said, "There is a town called Little Rock about two miles from here so I think I will ride in and see if there is a wire at the telegraph office from Wes Montana and maybe Cheyenne.

I will be back as soon as I can and just stay alert. And of course say close to the wagon." He said, "You know next Thursday is Thanksgiving so maybe I could find two turkeys in town and we could have turkey for Thanksgiving. They all agreed that would be great, and told Shermon if he could find any cranberry sauce to get it also. Shermon said, "Like I said I won't be gone very long." but then he told them that he was real proud of them. "Well I suppose we will have fish for supper so I will be back before supper time."

When Shermon reached town he first went to the telegraph office and ask the clerk if there was a telegraph for Shermon McBay? The clerk said, "Wow you are Shermon McBay?" Shermon said that he was Shermon McBay and asked if there was a problem. The clerk said, "No problem sir, there is two wires here for you. One from Wes Montana and one from a Cheyenne Decker. Would you like for me to read them to you?" Shermon said, "No thanks. I'm sure you've already read them once. Just hand them to me and I will read them. The clerk said yes Mr. McBay. Do you want to send one back?" Shermon said, "I will let you know."

The first one from Cheyenne said that she was glad to hear that Wes and Harry had made it in time to help with the gun play, and she knew there was no play in "gun play". She would be waiting to see him and his family. The second one was from Wes Montana. West said that he explained the gunfight to Cheyenne. Then he said. "Good news Sherm, your name has been cleared in the gunfight with the three Reams. The Marshall has sent the wire to Utal Wilson in Missouri, and told him it was a fair fight on your part, that the Reams came gunning for you. The Marshall here in Oklahoma had wanted posters on Zach Reams and three of his other Gunslingers and he thought he would find wanted posters on the other four. West said that him and Harry received a very large reward on the four with wanted posters and that the Marshall said if he came up with any rewards on the other four, that he would send them to us. Shermon, Harry and me gave the Marshall the horses and saddles for the cost of the gunfighters to be buried on the hill. After reading the rest of the wire, Shermon headed to the General Store.

CHAPTER 18
SHERMON RETURNS WITH TWO TURKEYS AND GOOD NEWS

Shermon asked the clerk at the General Store if they might have a turkey or two, and fixings for a turkey dinner. The clerk told Shermon that there was a place down the road that raised turkeys, but he wasn't sure if they had any left. Then the clerk said, "I might have a few items that you might be interested in. Shermon asked, "What do you have?" The clerk said, I have some yams, spud potatoes, cranberry sauce, and some ready-made dressing in a box." Shermon said, "Any pumpkin pie?" The clerk said, "We have some pumpkin in a can." Shermon said he would take the pumpkin in the can plus the yams and two large bags of potatoes, and of course, the cranberry sauce and a whole bag of onions. The clerk said, "Good is there anything else?" Shermon said, "Yeah, where did you say that turkey farm was?" The clerk said follow the road to the end of town, go right and you'll run into the Becker place, it's the place with a porch all the way across the front and a white picket fence. You can't miss it."

Shermon said, "Well, if you let me know how much I owe you and pack the items up so I can carry them on the back of my horse, I will go see about that turkey." Shermon paid the clerk, and then left for the Becker place. Shermon met Bill Becker, and told him that he would like to buy at least one turkey and maybe two if possible for his family as they were on a trail outside of town. Bill's wife walked up as Shermon was telling Bill about Shermon and his family heading to Waco Texas from Kansas Missouri. Then Shermon told marry the same story that he had just told Bill and also that he was trying to surprise them with the turkeys. Mary said, "Bill, there is ducks flying outside of the river over there, and you just said that you would like to shoot some and that you had a taste for duck. Why don't you shoot three or four of them ducks and we can have duck for Thanksgiving dinner?" Bill said, "You know Mary that is a great idea! I would much rather have ducks for Thanksgiving than turkeys. Bill then asked Shermon, "Is two turkeys enough?   Shermon said, "Yes it would be plenty."

Shermon then said, "If you are sure that you want to sell me your last two turkeys, just let me know how much I owe you." Mary said, "Shermon, me and Bill want to give those two turkeys to you and your family." Shermon said "I will be happy to pay for those two turkeys." Bill said "Shermon, Mary and me won't sell them to you but we will give them to you and your family for Thanksgiving. Shermon you can just tie them turkeys behind your horse and they will run all day if they need to. They can't fly very fast but they can run real fast and forever." Shermon thanked the Becker's for the two turkeys and said, "We'll just tie them on a long lease behind Buck," and then he rolled out of town with his Thanksgiving dinner.

As Shermon rode into camp, he asked Lance to help him tie the two turkeys to a tree. Shermon said, "Buck will sure be glad to be rid of them two birds." Reminton said, "Those sure are too large turkeys and it looks like Rusty would like to get a hold of them birds." Shermon said, "We will have to dress them Birds ASAP." Dakota said, "Uncle Sherm I caught the biggest fish that I have ever seen. Uncle Reminton had to help me get it in." Reminton said, "Sherm that trout was over ten pounds and it was a big brown trout!" Then Abigail said, "And it's ready to eat if you are Shermon?"

Shermon said, "Let me just unload these fixins, and wash my face and hands." Then Shermon walked back to the fire and KaSandra handed Sher-mon a hot tin cup full of hot, black coffee. After a real good meal Reminton asked, "Where did you find them turkeys Sherm?" Shermon said, "I tried to buy them but Bill and Mary Becker had them and would not sell them, but they told me they would give them to me and they did. Then I bought the other fixin's at the General Store." Brandy said, "I know we just ate but these turkeys are making me hungry." Shermon said, "We will hobble their legs and keep them tied up until we can butcher them." Then they saw Valerie throwing breadcrumbs to the turkeys, and Rusty kept the turkeys at bay.

They all laughed at Rusty and then Valerie led Rusty away from the turkeys. Reminton asked, "Was there any wires for you at the telegraph office Sherm?" Shermon said, "There were two, one from Wes Montana, and one from Cheyenne Decker." KaSandra said, "Tell us what Cheyenne's wire said first Shermon." Shermon said, "Cheyenne said she was sorry that my brother Lance got shot, and she hoped he was okay, and that she was happy no one else got hurt." Dakota said, "What about your ear Uncle Sherm?"

Shermon said, "Cheyenne did say that Montana had mentioned my ear, and Cheyenne did say that even with only a half of an ear she thought that she would be able to be seen with me in public." Valerie said, "Uncle Sherm, your hair hides your ears so you would have to tie your hair back if you want them to see your ears". Shermon laughed the same as the others did and then said, "I think I will leave my hair the way it is and not tie it back." They laughed again then Reminton asked, "Did Wes Montana say anything about Zach Reams and the other gunslingers?"

"Well first, it was said that I was cleared." They all said they were really glad to hear that Shermon was cleared about the shooting of the three Reams. Wyatt asked, "What did Wes Montana have to say about Zack Reams and his Gunslingers?" Valerie asked, "Don't you mean the buzzard meat?" Brandy asked, "Where did you get such a name Valerie, as buzzard meat?" Valerie said, "Uncle Sherm said that they should leave them for buzzard meat. Uncle Sherm said it to Uncle Reminton and to Wes Montana." Sherm said, "Brandy, Valerie is right. I said we could leave them for buzzard meat, but Wes and Harry took them to the Marshall in Oklahoma and left their horses saddles and guns for payment, which buried the eight fellows on the hill.

With eight small headstones that were bought with the reward money that Zach Reams had on his head. That is also when my name was cleared. There was Wes Montana, Harry Austin and at least a half dozen other men that testified that the shooting of the three Reams was a fair fight, and that I had no

choice, it was either them or me.

CHAPTER 19
SHERMON TELLS ABOUT HIS TIME WITH THE APACHES.

KaSandra said as she was trying not to cry, "Shermon, we all are very happy that your name was cleared, and we thanked God many times for returning you to us." Then Reminton said, "Sherm, what KaSandra is trying to say is how much we love you and how glad we are that we have you. We know that you will talk to us about your capture when you are ready, but we also know that maybe you would rather not." Shermon said, "Well, tomorrow is Sunday, so how about I tell you what I can after breakfast? For now, I think we should get some sleep."

The next morning after a real good breakfast, Shermon said, "Last night's trout fish dinner and this morning's breakfast was really something to be thankful for." After a short pause Shermon continued. "Well, first I guess I will say, there were people who cried to themselves every night, but tried not to cry out loud to where they would be heard by the Indians. There were people who wanted to be given a knife so they could end their miserable and painful life.

Every captive had to work all day and then was tied up every night. There was this one guy that a couple of the braves caught watching the squaws bathing in the stream. The squaws were naked and washing and splashing around in the water. Then they started screaming when they saw the guy watching them. The Indians figured that they needed to see to it that the guy could never sneak around and watch their squaws bathe again, so they cut the guy's eyelids completely off where he could never close his eyes again, and then they staked him in the direct sunlight. After a few days, the guy went crazy.

The Indians then covered the guy with animal blood all over his naked body, then tied him to the side of the cliff. The guy kept screaming while he was being attacked and slowly eaten by vultures. That is the largest bird of prey, with large naked red heads and very long beaks that are very sharp and horny and they tear very deep holes into their prey. The guy was praying to die, and finally did but only after many days and nights."

Shermon continued, "They brought in a woman with a small girl maybe eight or nine years old. The braves repeatedly had their way with the woman as her little girl watched. Even after the woman passed out, the braves still took turns with the woman. Finally the woman killed herself one night or she just died, and the little girl cried and screamed like she had went crazy.

The Indians thought the little girl had really gone crazy, and Indians do not want anything to do with a crazy person! The Indians cut the little girl loose, and the little girl ran right through the fire and then jumped off the rocky cliff to her grave."

KaSandra and the others asked Shermon, how could the Indians be so cruel?" Shermon said, "Somehow I don't think the Indians think they are being cruel, I just don't think they know any better." Then he said, "I saw many other bad things happen while I was held captive, and that is why I say I was lucky. I will probably never forget any of it, but I would like to try to forget what I can. I have learned that Indians can be very cruel."

CHAPTER 20
THE THANKSGIVING DINNER

Shermon's whole family was in tears and said they did understand what he meant when he said he was lucky, and only with God's help did he survive. Shermon said, "Well, I would like to grease them wagon wheels and check that front wheel on the third wagon. Then I'd like to rest a while and call it a night."

The next morning Shermon said, "That was a real good breakfast and I would like some more coffee." Everyone in Shermons family jumped up and said, "I will get it!" Shermon said, "I will get it myself but I want to thank everyone just the same." Then Shermon said, "How about we rest the rest of today and then get an early start in the morning? Tomorrow will be Monday then after a couple more days it will be Thanksgiving the next day."

So then Wednesday came and Shermon said, "I will be up front a little ways. We made real good time these last couple of days, so we'll set up camp tonight and have a great thanksgiving meal tomorrow. I know everyone is eager, but still stay alert!"

Later that day they seen Shermon sitting on Buck. When they reached Shermon, he said, "I know it's still a little early for night camp, but I don't think we will find a better place than right up ahead. There's plenty of water, deadwood and grass on the side of a little knoll."

After they made camp, Reminton said, "There is ducks flying in and out of them cat tails."Shermon asked Dakota and Logan to help him gather some deadwood and dried buffalo chips. Then Shermon said, "Let's have a little grub and call it a night." And they did.

The next morning Reminton said, "I am going to get some duck eggs," and he asked Wyatt to go with him. Shermon said, "Me and these two young men will prepare the two turkeys." Lance said, "I will add fuel to the fire and help the women with whatever they might need." Shermon said, "That sounds real good."

Shermon said, "We'll pluck these birds and get them ready." As they got the turkeys ready, Reminton and Wyatt had some real nice duck eggs. KaSandra said, "I will take those eggs. We have biscuits ready. Will biscuits, duck eggs and smoked bacon be good? Of course the coffe is also ready."

Again Shermon said how good the breakfast was and he thought he would scout around the campsite a little. Reminton asked, "Ok if I go with you Sherm?" Shermon said, "Sure, let's go." The he said, "We won't be more that maybe three to four hundred feet from camp, so keep your guard up and we will be back real soon." The women were working on the fixens, and Lance with Wyatt's help was putting the two turkeys on a spit at the fire. Lance noticed the girls chasing a bird and told them not to leave camp while chasing the bird. When Shermon and Reminton returned, the girls told them about the bird that sounded like a cat.

Shermon asked, "Was it a white bird with black wings and a black head?" The girls said it was and it meowed like a cat. Shermon said it was a Cat bird or anyway it was called a Cat bird. Shermon walked over to the fire and sat on his heels and poured himself a cup of coffee. Lance asked, "Well Sherm, did you and Reminton see anything out there?" Shermon said, "There was some tracks and I believe they were mostly Navajo tracks."

Wyatt asked, "Did you trail them Sherm?" Shermon said, "Well, we stayed back some and watched the trail, but I have learned you never follow Indians into the woods or over a hillside. Dakota asked, "Why not Uncle Sherm?" Shermon said, "That is a real good question code man. You see you can almost always bet that there will be more Indians waiting behind trees, or over on the other side of the hill, and that's what they want you to do, is follow or chase them into the woods. Remember it is always better to pick your own fight, and fight your own fight, and not theirs. I want to add that it's always okay to avoid a fight when you can!"

Shermon seen that everyone was listening to him so he said, "Let's try not to worry and pay a bill before it's due! Let's enjoy Thanksgiving. KaSandra called, "Dinner is ready!" As they walked towards the fire, Dakota asked, "When are we going to use that dinner bell we bought before we left Kansas City?" Shermon said, "We bought it to use in Waco and when we use it, we will see the lettering which says Kansas City, Missouri. We will always remember where it all started."

Dakota said, "Yeah, that's a good idea we had." KaSandra said, "We have carved the two turkeys, and we put the white meat in this pan and all the dark meat in this other pan next to where you are Shermon because we know you like the dark meat."

Shermon said, "That's right, I do prefer the dark but there is way too much for me." Dakota said, "I will eat one of those turkey legs uncle Sherm." Shermon said, "Dakota, you can have all four, if you can eat them!" Dakota said, "I can't eat all four, but I can eat one." Brandy said, "We also have sweet yams, potatoes, cranberry sauce, ready-made dressing, plus biscuits, and not only hot coffee, but we also have hot tea!"

KaSandra said, "And you need to save room for blackberry pie. We found the berries and made pie in the dutch oven. Shermon said, "I have seen a lot of farkle berries, but I did not see the black berries." Brandy said, "We found the blackberry bushes and we only ate a few." Shermon said, "Well I'm glad you saved enough for that large pie, so I guess I will have a piece." Valerie asked, "Uncle Sherm, are farkle berries good to eat?"

Uncle Shermon said, "No, Valerie. farkle berries are not good to eat. They grow on a short tree, or bush, and they have small while bell shaped flowers. The berries are small and hard, and purple to black in color." Logan then asked, "Is that the only way to tell that they are no good?" Shermon said, "The best way to tell if anything is good or not, is to watch if the birds or other animals are eating any. If the birds or other animals aren't eating it, you can bet it's no good, and you don't want to eat it!" Then he said, "I am so full, I know you women are surely going to make me fat!" KaSandra said, 'Shermon, you will never be fat! I'll bet on it!"

Shermon said, "I will if I keep eating like this, but I am glad you brought that dutch oven." He continued, "Looks like Rusty likes black berry pie also!" They all looked and Rusty had his big head in the dutch oven. KaSandra said, "Good thing we were done with that pie because Rusty is finishing it off.

Shermon said, "Well, it's been a good day, and what a meal we just had!" Let's drag over some more of that deadwood closer to the fire, and then maybe we should try to get some shut eye. I think we should double the night guard. I don't want to worry anyone, and I'm sure we won't have any trouble tonight, but that water over there is called sweet water, and that puts us in Indian territory, so let's keep our guard up and have a gun ready at all times. I believe the water is called sweet water because of all the black berries. Well, let's get some shut eye."

The next morning, Shermon said, "Well, the night went good, but I feel a little uneasy, so, let's eat some breakfast and break camp. I will take the lead, but I will stay close."

CHAPTER 21
THE NAVAJOS ATTACK, BUT THE MCBAYS HAVE HELP

Shermon said as he was heading out to scout, "Stay close to the wagons." Shermon was a little worried about the feeling he had, but he did not want to worry his family. It wasn't very long when Reminton said, "You hear the shooting up ahead? The Indians have Shermon pinned down in the rocks up ahead!" Dakota said, "We have to ride out and help uncle Shermon." Lance said, "Look there are thirty or more heading our way!"

Reminton yelled, "Pull the wagons in a triangle, we're going to be attacked!" Lance said, "Dakota, you and Logan take cover. Uncle Sherm will be all right. We have to stay with the wagons." Reminton yelled, "Get ready, take cover, and get ready to shoot." Then Wyatt said, "Look at Shermon, he is charging the Indians like he has an army behind him." Then Lance said, "Look out," and there was Navajos all around them.

Dakota said, "I hope uncle Sherm will be ok, he is trying to get to us." Reminton said, "Uncle Shermon is worried about us, so start shooting." Lance yelled, "Look at all those Indians coming up behind Shermon. I think those Indians are Apaches. They look different from these." Then an arrow hit right between Lance and Reminton, and the fight was on!

Reminton noticed that the Indians had split up, maybe a dozen rode towards Shermon, and the rest was headed toward the three wagons. Shermon was charging the Navajo, and they did not see the ten or more Apaches also heading toward them. Shermon had already shot four of the Navajos and had yelled to the Apaches, "My family needs help," and that is why most of the Apaches headed toward the three wagons. Geronimo lifted up his war lance and the hills opened up with Apaches to help the small wagon train.

Shermon had both his 44 colts in his hands when he and Buck reached the small wagon train. Shermon pulled his triggers and the two Navajos fell to the ground. Then Shermon shot another one that was trying to stick Reminton with a bowie knife, and then Reminton shot a Navajo that was trying to sneak up on Shermon.

Katelyn was yelling because there was a Navajo trying to drag her to his horse by her hair. Dakota shot the Indian that had a hold on Katelyn's hair, and then fired again and shot one that was climbing up the back of the wagon that Valerie was hiding in. Then Dakota seen Rusty jump from the wagon and knock an Indian to the ground, but the Navajo pulled a boot knife and stabbed Rusty as Rusty got on top of the Navajo.

Reminton yelled, "KaSandra needs help," as he was fighting with an Indian and trying to finish him off. Then Shermon and Reminton both reached the wagon at about the same time. KaSandra had an arrow in her, and was fighting with a Navajo who was trying to take her blonde hair. The Indian was on top of her, getting ready to take her hair, when Shermon and Reminton both put a bullet in him. Then Shermon knocked the Indian off of KaSandra.

The blood from the Indian that Shermon and Reminton had shot, had spattered all over KaSandra, but KaSandra stood right up any way for a second, but then she fell right into Reminton's arms. KaSandra had an arrow in her upper chest and she had blood everywhere, on her and on the Indian that Shermon and Reminton had just shot. Shermon climbed down from the wagon, and Dakota was standing firm with a colt 44 in one hand and he was putting 44 shells into it. Shermon said, "Good job code man. Stand watch, I will be back." Then Lance said, "Sit down Wyatt, before you fall." Wyatt was also covered in blood.

Brandy was at the back of the wagon with a look on her face that Shermon was not sure about. Shermon knew that Valerie was in there so without saying anything, Shermon just climbed into the wagon. Shermon saw Valerie. She was crying hard, but she was ok. Also in the wagon, there was three dead Indians. Shermon hugged Valerie. He was happy to see her and to know her mom was ok. He said, "You did a good job Brandy," and hugged her. Then Abigail yelled, and Shermon jumped out of the wagon to see what she was screaming about.

Shermon had both of his colts pulled. Logan had an arrow sticking in his upper thigh. Shermon grabbed Logan, just as he was falling. Shermon said something under his breath and sat Logan next to where Reminton had just sat KaSandra. Then Shermon said, "Lance, help Wyatt over here, next to Logan." Reminton said, "Sherm, you have been hit also." Shermom said, "It's just a scratch." Shermon then said, "Lance start a fire, and Dakota will you get a couple of those sticks over there? Try to get straight ones if you can." Then Shermon asked Reminton to cut the powder out of four 44 shells.

Lance gathered some buffalo chips and built a nice, small fire. Dakota said, "I have some real nice sticks here." Reminton had four different powder loads. Shermon broke off the arrow head on the arrow in KaSandra's chest, plus the one in Logan's leg. KaSandra was in some pain, but handled it well, and Logan was passed out. Shermon said, "KaSandra, this is going to hurt but it has to be done." KaSandra said, "Go ahead Shermon. I'm ready."

Shermon cut the shaft in a notch and poured the gun powder in, then lit it and shoved the arrow through. KaSandra barely let out a sound. All the Apaches were impressed. Then Shermon did the same with Logan's leg. Logan was passed out and did not move or make a sound. Then Shermon moved to Wyatt. Wyatt was bleeding, but the bullet had gone right through. Shermon poured some gun powder into Wyatt's wound and said, "Wyatt this is going to hurt some."

Wyatt said, "Go ahead big brother, and I will try to be as brave as KaSandra," then he laughed. Wyatt did not laugh long, because Shermon lit the gun powder and the flame shoot through Wyatt's wound, and Wyatt almost bit a hole through his lip, but Wyatt made almost no sound.

The Apaches were impressed and said, "The big man is strong, like the woman is strong. Shermon asked Wyatt, "How do you feel?" Wyatt said, "Like you said Sherm, lucky I think." Shermon said, "Well, I'm sure we all were very lucky, thanks to God and the Apaches. Now I had better look at Rusty and see how bad that Indian stuck him."

Shermon moved over to Rusty. He said, "Let's have a look at you Rusty." At first, Shermon was worried but after he took a good look at Rusty, he said, "Rusty, I guess you were lucky also because I was thinking that maybe you got gut stuck, but you have just a little skin and hair gone. You are a real good warrior dog, Rusty. "Valerie and Katelyn were crying, but they were happy that Rusty wasn't hurt too bad. Dakota said, "Good dog Rusty, and looked away.

Shermon was sweating, but he was also bleeding, because his buckskin pants were really stained. Shermon said, "Reminton, bring the rest of that gun powder over here, and Dakota stick one of them sticks in the fire." Shermon cut his right pant leg about knee high and said, "There is the bullet, it almost made it through." Shermon removed the bullet, and handed it to Dakota. Then Shermon said, "Rem., let me have that gunpowder," and poured the gun powder in the hole and then lit it. The flame shot through his leg, and the bleeding stopped. Shermon said, "Is there coffee in that pot, and took himself a cup and after he drank it, he looked around. He said, "Well, that's that, I guess.

Shermon got up and walked over to KaSandra and hugged her. He then walked over to Logan and looked at his leg. He stepped over to Wyatt and looked at Wyatt's injury. Shermon looked all around at the rest of his family, and Shermon's chest was swollen with pride. Shermon said, "I am so proud of you all, and you are all warriors. We might not have made it without Geronimo and his braves, but like I said I could not be more proud of my family. I am sorry that you KaSandra, Wyatt, and Logan got hurt, and I'm sorry that Rusty also got hurt plus I'm sorry that you had to go through this."

They told Shermon this was not his fault and he took an awful big chance out there his self. Then Geronimo stepped up to Shermon and said, "Your family are all great warriors and you are a lucky man to have this great family, just as they are lucky to have you." Shermon said, "Yes Geronimo, I am very lucky." Dakota said, "Look Geronimo is as big as Uncle Sherm." Then Shermon said, "Geronimo, I want to thank you for helping me and my family." Geronimo said, "We are brothers."

The rest of the McBays did not understand all the words that Geronimo and Shermon spoke, but they knew it was good because he had that swollen chest, and you could not deny the handshake. They shook hands and Shermon grasp Geronimo's forearm and Geronimo grasp Shermon's forearm.

KaSandra moved a little and felt the pain but she did not make a sound. Brandy said, "There is coffee ready if you want any Sherm." Dakota said, "I think I will have a cup, because this Indian fighting is tough." He looked at Geronimo after he said it. Shermon said, "Dakota, you did real good, so Brandy why don't you let Dakota have the first cup while I step out with Geronimo for a minute." Geronimo said, "You surely are a great white Warrior, and your family are warriors also." Then Geronimo said, "I am sorry that we did not get here sooner. We were tracking the Navajos when we heard the shooting.

Shermon said, "Geronimo my family and me would not have made it without your braves." Geronimo said, "We have gathered up the Navajo horses and we have many scalps for our teepee poles." They cleaned up and they thanked God and the Apaches to be alive. Reminton asked Shermon if he saw what the Apaches did to the Navajos. Remington said, the Apache scalped them, and poked out their eyes. Sherman said, yes the Apaches took the Navajos scalps for their teepee poles.

The Indians believe that taking the scalps and hanging them on their teepee poles or lodge poles give them great power. Shermon then said they poked out their eyes so they can't find their way to the happy hunting-grounds. Shermon saw Brandy looking in the wagon and said, "There are no more dead Indians in that wagon are there Brandy?"

Brandy said, "No, the Apaches drug them away with the rest." Sherman asked, "How did you happen to have three Navajos in your wagon Brandy?" Brandy said, "I saw Wyatt get shot and then the Indian was trying to stick him with a large knife when you rode in and put two bullets in the Indian. It was the same time that KaSandra dropped two Indians at the front of the wagon she was in. When three Indians decided to come in the back of my wagon, as they came in I shot them one by one."

Then KaSandra took an arrow, but she still shot the Navajo off his horse even after she got stuck with the arrow. Then Logan started to come to and Shermon asked, "How are you doing Logan?" Logan said, "My leg really hurts, but I'm alive and that sure is better than being dead, right?" Shermon said, "It sure is Logan. Then Logan said with a little shaking in his voice, "Uncle Sherm, I thought for sure we were all going to die, but I know I got two of those Navajos."

Shermon said, "You did real good Logan." KaSandra said, "Sherm we all know how bad you feel, but this was not your fault, and we could never have made it this far without you. Shermon we all voted to go to Waco and we still want to." Shermon said, "Well at least I thank God that none of us died, but I can't help feeling bad and I also know that time will heal us."

Reminton said, "Shermon there is a large tear in the bonnet of the first wagon." Reminton was trying to get Shermon's mind off what had just happened, and it seemed to work because Shermon said, "We could switch the bonnet on the third wagon with the bonnet on the first. That water barrel on the second wagon is done for sure. We can use the wood and keep the metal band and we can replace that water barrel with one of the extra ones we have."

Brandy said, "Shermon, I›m sure me and Abigail can mend that torn bonnet enough to cover the tools and water in the third wagon" Shermon said, "Go ahead and see what you can do, but I wouldn›t put too much work on it. We will move the beans, and whatever dry goods that is in the third wagon, and split them up in the first and second wagon, and if there is anything that we take from the first and second we can put into the third wagon. Let's do that. Shermon then said, "Well all in all, we have a lot to be thankful for."

"We saved the wagons and stock, plus no one got killed that was in our small group." Dakota said, "It looked like them Navajos had plenty of horses, and why would they want our oxen? They wouldn't ride them would they?" Shermon replied, "No Dakota, but if they didn't eat them, they'd trade them to others for guns, blankets and anything else they might want." Valerie said, "They would eat are animals?" Shermon said, "They sure would. They would eat the oxen first, and then they would eat our horses, if they were hungry." Shermon continued, "Well like I said, I could not be more proud, and I am glad no one left the wagons!"

KaSandra said, "Shermon when we saw those Navajos cut you off and you took cover in those large rocks, we wanted to come out and help you. We even knew we should not leave the wagon train. I have to say we were going to head out to help you." Shermon said, "Well I am glad no one left the wagons. You see Indians are very clever. They wanted to pull you away from the cover of the wagons if they could. KaSandra said, "We knew that you would be worried about us, when you needed to be more worried about yourself out there! The way you charged those Indians. We said only Shermon would charge six Indians and not be worried about being killed.

Shermon said, "You all are great Indian fighters and all I was thinking of was getting to the wagons where I could help my family." KaSandra said, "Sure we all agreed that we don't want to do anything without you. We don't want you to take any unnecessary chances, okay Sherm?" Shermon said, I'll try to be careful but sometimes I react without thinking first, I guess."

Shermon then said, "You see, the Indians only know how to be chargers. They don't know how to be the chargee. Indians lose their edge, and most of the time they lose their nerve when anything happens that they don't understand, or is very different than what they are used to." Reminton said, "We all have agreed that you are the Indian fighter, and you know their ways and their speech. We need you and we are so very proud of you and we don't want you to take any unnecessary chances, ok?"

Shermon said, "Thank you, thank you very much. I will do my best and try to think before I jump!" Then Shermon said, "I hate to remind you that we are in real Indian Territory now, so let's be careful. I'm sure we will be fine. Let's make camp over there by that stream because today is almost gone. I will take some black coffee now and maybe a biscuit or two. I will be over there on that rise so you will be between me and the water. It will be nightfall soon, so try to get some shut eye, and keep your guard up. I have noticed some of Geronimo's braves in the area, so it looks like we will have extra guards tonight. There are seven or eight across that creek. I see three or four fires, so it looks like they are setting a few camps. Like I said, I will be back soon. Then Shermon rode out on Buck.

"I hate that Shermon is taking this so bad." Lance said, "Well, I guess Sherm just needs a little time to himself." Wyatt said, "You know that anything that happens that is bad in anyway, Shermon blames himself!" Reminton said, "Well, I hope that we can change that some, and I think that we should try!"

Shermon rode back into camp and said, "I see you have the privy up and a real nice fire going. It looks like everyone is ready for some shuteye. That's good. We have quite a few of Geronimo's braves close, but let's keep our own night watch also."

They set up night watch, and the next morning the McBays camp was coming awake, Shermon was sitting at the fire, sitting on his heels pouring coffee in his tin cup. Shermon said, "It looks like the Apaches pulled out at sun up and it also looks like it is going to be a beautiful day. We are making good time. I think we should be in Waco in about six or seven weeks. How's everyone feeling this morning?"

KaSandra said. "Sherm, I think the rest of us feel fine, and we are ready for about anything. How are you feeling?" Shermon said, "I think I would have to be twins to feel any better," and he laughed a little. Logan asked," Uncle Sherm, how do you know so much about removing arrows and bullets?" Shermon said, "Logan, I have been scouting for quite a few years, and through all of those years I have removed a few from other folks as well as myself."

Logan asked, "What's better, when the arrow is sticking threw or not sticking out?" Shermon said, "It is much better when the arrow head is threw, because if it's not through, you have to push it through, and believe me, that arrow head hurts real bad when it is pushed through! When the arrow is sticking through, you cut off the arrowhead and then cut a groove in the shaft of the arrow, fill it with gun powder, light it and shove it through. It hurts real bad but then you should not bleed to death because your wound has been cauterized."

They all ate a good breakfast and then Shermon said, "Should we break camp and put some miles behind us and get closer to Waco?" They said, "We are ready." Shermon said, "There's a nice breeze pushing us, so let's just head out and see how many miles we can make." Shermon said, "What's a matter Buck, you sure act like something is bothering you?" Shermon then said, "Let's roll on out. He said to Buck as they started out, "You sure are feeling uneasy Buck, the same as me. Buck you are one heck of a horse! My family does not know how much I talk to you, but a lot of the time I only talk to you.

It's just you and me. As long as you don't mind, I will just keep talking to you. You might not understand everything that I say, but I know you understand what matters the most. They are all watching the skies, the same as we are Buck, so let's not get too far ahead. The temperature is really dropping and the wind acts like it does not know which way to blow." Shermon said, "Buck look at them tree tops blowing, and them clouds are moving so fast and it's getting so dark so fast!"

CHAPTER 22
THE TORNADO

Reminton said to Lance, "The last five miles or so, the weather has been really turning for the worse, and I don't see any end to it." Lance said, "Look, there's Shermon and he is riding hard!" Lance said, "It looks like Shermon is telling us to pull off to the right, and he's motioning for us to do it as fast as we can!" Reminton yelled as they were pulling off the trail, "Look at that large funnel cloud. It's on the ground and it looks like it is not moving because it is heading right for us!"

The wind was howling and the skies were turning black. Reminton yelled, "Hurry, pull towards that valley. We need to get as low as we can." Wyatt said, "Rem, them oxen are doing the best they can. Let's unhook the remuda and hope they head toward Shermon." Lance said, "This violent whirlwind is the worst I've ever seen, but let's not let it get the best of us."Reminton said, "We have to make it to the valley."

The clouds were rotating rapidly, and the trees were being uprooted. Shermon was still waving and yelling, and trying to make himself heard over the loud thunder. "Come on," he said, "Don't let this hundred mile wind beat us!" With Shermon in the lead, they pulled as close to the hillside as possible. Shermon yelled, "Get as close to this bluff as you can!"

KaSandra said, "The noise is so loud, and the trees are being uprooted. I have never seen the clouds go in four different directions at the same time!" Brandy yelled,"Look, that tall grass is almost laying out flat!" Then Abigail said, "There goes the bonnet on the third wagon!" Reminton yelled, "I know it's too late, but I wish that we had gotten down a little farther." KaSandra yelled, "If you can hear me over this rain, I have never seen it rain this hard, or the wind be so loud." Shermon yelled, "Hold tight and stay down, it will let up soon!"

No sooner than Shermon said it, it started to let up. The rain had let up and the wind was not blowing that hard anymore. Reminton said, "Well it looks like that third wagon is beyond repair. That tree landed right on top of it. The water barrel and the jockey box is busted up also and the tongue and neck is twisted beyond repair."

Shermon said, "Yeah, it took out that wagon, but at least we got the oxen unhooked or they would have been under that tree also!" KaSandra said, thank the Lord, the rain is letting up and the wind is also letting up!" Shermon said, "Well, it looks like the worst is over! I think we should pull the other two wagons over where we can put up the large dinner tarp, and we can use a couple of these trees to help attach the dinner tarp. It looks like the rain is going to go on through the night, so we will get the tarp up and make a fire. We'll take care of that wagon in the morning."

Reminton said, "We have plenty of dead wood and buffalo chips that we have accumulated along the trail." KaSandra said, "Sherm, like you always say, I guess it could have been worse!" Then she said, "Dinner is ready."

Shermon sat on his heels at the fire and poured himself a cup of coffee then said, "Yeah KaSandra, I guess it could have been much worse!" Then he said, "Let's have some grub and then we will set up night camp."

After a great meal, Shermon said, "It seems like no matter what we go through, there's always a great meal to be had." The privy was set up, and Shermon reminded everyone that no one should go to the privy without a guard, and said, "I don't want to worry anyone but we are still in Indian country."

The next morning, Shermon sat on his heels at the fire pouring his self a cup of coffee. He said, "Well that third wagon is no more than fire wood, but

I thank God that all three wagons weren't destroyed! Let's put what we can from the third wagon in to the first and second, but still save whatever floor space we can. It looks like we can save both wheels on the left side of the wagon, the small one on the front and the large one on the back. I think we should. Hopefully, we won't need them, but we might keep them a while. We will just fasten them to the second wagon. With the rain letting up, the trail should dry out fast and we can head out tomorrow."

Reminton said, "Well there is plenty of room under and on the sides of the second wagon where we can put the wood from the third wagon." Shermon said, "That's a great idea! I guess we could do the same with the first wagon if we had to. Let's top off the water barrels and save as much of the bonnet as we can, in case we need to make a repair." Then Shermon said, "Well, it's been a long day. Time flies when you are having fun." Then he laughed. He continued, "The oxen have eaten their fill of the grass, and the horses are content, so what do you say, let's get some shut eye for ourselves. We should be fine, but listen and be ready for anything." Reminton said, "Lance said, okay, I will take the first watch," and Lance said, "I will replace you in a couple of hours."

In the morning Shermon said, "KaSandra, I thought my watch had just started when you said the biscuits were ready! I could sure use a biscuit and look at this thick smoked bacon, and those beans." Then KaSandra handed Shermon a tin cup with hot black coffee and Shermon said, "Who could ask for more!"

Wyatt said, "Shermon, I want to get to Waco same as everyone else, but I sure am having trouble getting motivated this morning." Shermon asked, "Are you feeling ok Wyatt?" Wyatt said, "Yes, but I think it is all this mud and only two wagons." Shermon asked, "Wyatt, you aren't ready to turn back are you?" Wyatt said, "No way!" Shermon said, "Wyatt, that muddy water running over there reminds me of back home, you know, the Missouri river, what everyone calls, The Big Muddy." Shermon then said, "We do need a third wagon and we are close to Eldorado and you would think that we could find a wagon there."

Wyatt asked, "Shermon would you really buy another wagon when we are so close?" Shermon said, "We still have a ways to go and we can get our money back when we sell it later." Wyatt said, "Well I hope it wasn't because of what I said?" Shermon said, "No Wyatt, we really can use another wagon. We will get back as much as we pay for it now."

Shermon said, "Well, it looks like a beautiful morning," and walked over and sat down and started whittling. Reminton said, "Shermon you sure have been doing a lot of whittling!"

Shermon said, "Well, Reminton I wanted to keep it a secret, but I am whittling a couple of wood dolls for Katelyn and Valerie for Christmas. I have made a couple of real nice sling shots for Dakota and Logan, plus it gives me time to think when I am whittling."

CHAPTER 23
THEY REACH ELDORADO AND SHERMON, REMINTON, AND KASANDRA GO TO TOWN.

Shermon said, "Well, I think that a couple of us should go to town while the rest stay close to camp" Reminton said, "Sherm, if you are okay with it, KaSandra and myself will go into town with you? You and me can look for a wagon and whatever else we need, and KaSandra needs to go to the general store."Shermon said, "That's fine with me. We will go right after we set up camp. Down by the water looks good to me."

They all agreed and decided that fish would be their meal, if they could catch enough for dinner. Dakota and Logan said that they would have plenty of fish for dinner. About that time KaSandra came around from the other side of the wagon and said, "Are you two cowboys ready, or should I go without you two?" KaSandra's long blonde hair was blowing slightly in the breeze. She had on a white button down shirt, with the top two buttons unbuttoned, revealing only the top of her breast, yet it was not too revealing. Her jeans fit her like socks on a turkey. Reminton said, "KaSandra, I think you would stop a twelve day clock with that outfit on."

KaSandra then asked, "Do I look ok?" Reminton and Shermon both said, "KaSandra you look fine." Then Shermon said, "KaSandra with that colt 44 on your one hip, and that skinning knife of your other, you look like you are ready to go to town." Reminton said, "KaSandra I saddled this horse that you like so much" The horse was about fifteen hands tall, with mostly dark markings. KaSandra even looked like she belonged on the horse.

Shermon said, "Lance you and Wyatt keep a rifle with you at all times, and the rest of you, stay alert." Lance said, "Shermon do you expect us to have trouble while you are gone?" Shermon said, "No, I don't but like I always say, be ready for anything." Then Shermon, Reminton and KaSandra rode out of camp. After watching the three ride away, Lance said, "Let's go catch lots of fish, and have some fun!"

Reminton told Shermon that KaSandra was very good with a rifle, and also with a colt 44. She had practiced until she could hit ten out of ten times. Reminton then said that he thought they looked really good to him. KaSandra and Reminton were on the two tall quarter horses, and Shermon on Buck, who was even a little taller than the two quarter horses. Then Reminton said, "But the best was how KaSandra looked with her blonde hair blowing in the breeze.

Kasandra said, "Thanks Reminton. I guess I should wear this outfit more often." Reminton said, "Kasandra, you always look good, but I like it when your hair blows in the light breeze, it's an added bonus. As they pulled into El Dorado, Shermon said, "Look, there is a covered wagon in front of the general store. It's smaller than our other two, but that should be ok." Reminton said, "It's probably for sale because it's not hooked to any animals."

KaSandra said, "While you cowboys check out the wagon, I am going to head into the general store." As Shermon and Reminton were checking the wagon from top to bottom, there were a couple of fellows checking KaSandra out from head to toe! When KaSandra walked into the general store, the two men followed her into the store.

Inside the general store, Kasandra was telling the clerk that she was looking for enough buckskin to make a large shirt, and a pair of pants. As the clerk was showing KaSandra the buckskin and some rawhide and thread to match, KaSandra picked up a large needle. The larger of the two men said, "Honey be careful with that needle because it's sharp, and I sure wouldn't want you to get hurt"

KaSandra acted as if she did not hear him. Outside, Shermon told Reminton, "I think this wagon will be fine, and the sign said to see the bartender across the street, so do you want to go see the bartender or check on KaSandra?" At first, Reminton did not want either of them to walk in on KaSandra while she was buying the buckskin, so Reminton said, "Let's go see the bartender."

At the saloon, Shermon told the bartender that him and Reminton was interested in the wagon. The bartender gave them a good price on it because he had no use for it. So they paid for the wagon, and as they were walking out Reminton said, "You know Sherm, we really could use some 44 cartridges. We have used most of what we started with." Shermon said, "Well if you think KaSandra is still busy over at the general store, let's go get some ammo next door at the gun shop.

Reminton stepped into the gun shop first and Shermon looked around. Then Sherman stepped in after everything else looked calm outside. Reminton said, "My name is Reminton McBay, and this big fellow is my brother Shermon. The man behind the counter said, "My name is Ed Harvey Jones. As he shook hands with Shermon, and Reminton, he said, "My friends call me E.J."

Shermon said, "Well E.J., we could use maybe four hundred 44longs if you have them." E.J. said, "I have them. They are reloads, and I will make you a real sweet deal on five hundred 44 longs." Shermon said, I have always been a little careful about buying reloads." E.J. said, "Shermon I have reloaded these myself, and I guarantee you won't have a misfire." Shermon said," E.J., as long as you have reloaded them all yourself, I will buy them. It looks like you knew what you were doing E.J." Shermon said, "I am very careful when it comes to reloads, and I have been reloading shells for a lot of years." So E.J. set ten boxes of fifty on the counter and Shermon paid E.J. and they were shaking hands and reaching for the shells.

Bob Self

CHAPTER 24
SHERMON SAID, "I CAN'T COTTON TO, AND I WON'T TOLERATE RUDE PEOPLE!"

Shermon reached for the 44 longs, when they heard a woman yell, "Get away from me." Reminton said, "Shermon, that's KaSandra!" Reminton ran out of the gun shop with Shermon right behind him, and E.J. was right behind Shermon. Reminton yelled at the man who was in front of the wagon. The man was holding his crotch with one hand and going for his gun with his other hand. The man's shirt was cut to ribbons because of KaSandra's skinning knife and the man was holding his crotch because KaSandra had just kicked him in his testicles. When Reminton got close to the man, the man went for his gun. Reminton hit him with a right cross that broke the man's jaw, and also knocked him out. But what caused KaSandra to scream was that the big man had come up behind KaSandra and when he grabbed her, she dropped her knife and the big man was trying to kiss her. He had taken KaSandra's 44 and was trying to control her with his other hand. KaSandra scratched the big man's face, and then he slapped her real hard.

KaSandra heard Shermon yell at the large man, and felt a little relieved that Shermon was there, but then she watched him drag the large man out of the wagon by his hair. After kicking him in his face, Shermon helped him up, then hit the large man with a right cross and then a left hook, followed by an uppercut that looked like it lifted the guy off his feet. Shermon then threw a right that hit the guy in his heart, and KaSandra was sure that his heart skipped a beat. The big guy did try to kick Shermon, but Shermon kicked the guys other leg out from under him.

As he was going back, Shermon hit the large man right in his throat, and the large ugly man was gasping for air. Then Shermon finished it by breaking the guy's jaw and then the ugly man started to pull his gun and Shermon said, "I hope you pull that gun, because I would like to end this by putting a couple of bullets in your heart. The man could hardly speak, but he said, "This isn't over. I will see you again," but he did not try for his gun. Shermon said, "If I see you again, I will shoot you on site.

Then KaSandra realized she had lost a couple of buttons. So she covered herself the best she could. Reminton came up to KaSandra, and hugged her and said, "It's okay honey. Are you okay?" She said, "I will be fine. Thanks to you and Shermon. Reminton put out his hand, and when Shermon took it, he said, "Thank you big brother."

Shermon walked over to KaSandra and hugged her, and then he said, "I'm really sorry that this happened, and that you got slapped so hard." KaSandra said, "I didn't even feel the slap when it happened, but I do now, and I'm a little embarrassed about my shirt being torn open when my buttons were ripped off. Shermon said, "Let's hook those two Quarter Horses to the wagon, and then you and KaSandra can ride back to camp on the wagon seat if you want to Reminton." Reminton said, "That sounds good to me"

Quite a few people from town came up and shook Shermon's hand and some even slapped him on his back. They were saying things like, Tyrell and his brother had never been put down before. Tyrell would not let this end and the Morgan brothers were bullies. Shermon said well that will be up to him, but I will not tolerate rude people.

Shermon continued, like I said I can't cotton to rude people. Shermon said after me and Reminton hook the two quarter horses up to the wagon, are you two McBays ready to ride out?" He then asked, "Are you okay KaSandra?" She said, "Yes I'm okay, but what about you, are you okay?" Shermon said,

"Yeah I'm okay, maybe you think that I was a little hard on Morgan, but they said he was a bully, and like I said I won't tolerate rude people." So then Sherman asked, "Do you two want to head back to camp?" Reminton and KaSandra both said let's head out. Then on the way back, Reminton said, "You know KaSandra, I sure am glad that Shermon is on our side. KaSandra said, "I sure am too but I thought he was going to beat that ugly man to death. I know Shermon had hoped that ugly guy would go for his gun."

At the camp KaSandra snuck the buckskin and rawhide over to where Abigail and Brandy were, and they almost gave it away when they saw KaSandra's face so red and swollen. Everyone was asking, what happened in town. They knew that Shermon had gotten into a fight, and they weren't sure about Reminton and KaSandra. Katelyn was asking her mom what happened to her face, and uncle Sherman had blood on him. KaSandra said, "I'm okay honey. Let me fix my shirt, and I will be out in a minute or so." Shermon and Reminton were trying to give KaSandra all the time she needed.

When Katelyn left the wagon, KaSandra set down, and the tears rolled down her face. Her face was really swollen, and she knew she had been more scared than she had let on. She was so thankful that Shermon and Reminton had been there. She remembered the strength of the big ugly man, and knew that she did not have a chance against him without her gun or knife, which the guy had already taken from her. She could not believe the beating that Shermon had put on the big ugly man. After a little praying, and thanking God that things were not any worse, KaSandra climbed out of the wagon. The men had all the tools and things moved, and dinner was ready.

The McBays sat down to eat, but no one could contain their questions anymore. Shermon or Reminton did not say anything because they wanted to let KaSandra have all the time she needed. Then KaSandra just started talking. She said, "There were these two ugly men. Reminton hit one man, and knocked him out with one punch. There was another man, a very large ugly man that was trying to kiss me and when I would not let him kiss me that is when the big ugly man slapped me in the face real hard." Brandy asked, "Then what happened? KaSandra said, "Well that's when he messed up, because he took on Shermon." Brandy asked, "What happened Sherm?" Shermon said, "Not much. Let's let KaSandra tell the story."

KaSandra said, "You bet I will tell it. I thought Shermon was going to beat the big ugly man to death." Dakota ask, "What happen? The only bruises I see on uncle Shermon are on his fist. Did you even get hit uncle›s Sherm?" KaSandra said, "The ugly man tried to hit Sherm. He even tried to kick him, but Shermon did all the hitting. The ugly man just hit the ground." Dakota said, "So what happened?"KaSandra said, "Well that guy tried to stick Shermon with my knife. Shermon was way too fast and Shermon was waiting for the ugly man.

Every time the big ugly man moved Shermon would hit him. Shermon hit the guy so hard in his chest that the guy's heart skipped a beat, and he was holding his chest when Shermon hit him in his windpipe. The big ugly guy was gasping for air, but Shermon still hit him with a straight right and then an uppercut and lifted him off his feet.

Shermon wasn't done yet. Shermon took out the knee of big, then broke big uglys jaw. Shermon told big ugly to go for his gun so he could put a couple of bullets in him. KaSandra continued, I guess big ugly was not as dumb as he looked, because he did not go for his gun. Then Shermon said, "I won't tolerate rude people, and Shermon then knocked out big ugly." Dakota said, "I wish I was there to see it." Logan said, "Me too." Shermon said, well it happened so let's eat and then try to get some shut-eye."

CHAPTER 25
THE MCBAYS ARE BACK ON THE TRAIL WITH THREE WAGONS AND ONE SICK OX

The next morning after an uneasy night, Shermon was sitting at the fire ring on his heels pouring himself a cup of coffee. KaSandra walked up and Shermon asked, "How did you sleep last night KaSandra?" She said, "I guess I slept off and on all night, and my face feels a little better." Shermon said, "Yeah, I sure am sorry that you got slapped." KaSandra said, "Sherm, you need not to feel sorry, you saved me from big ugly. If you and Reminton weren't there, I don't want to think of what would have happened."

"Well, I only wish I had gotten there sooner KaSandra, "Shermon said. Then Reminton walked up and kissed KaSandra and told her that her face was just a little swollen, but she sure was pretty. KaSandra said, "Thanks Rem."

Shermon then said, "The weather sure looks good today, and now with three wagons again, I think we should gather as much buffalo chips and dead wood as we can so we can get back on the trail. There's water up ahead but we will find little dead wood."

Reminton said, "Sherm, I noticed that one of the oxen doesn't look so good." Shermon said, "I noticed the same thing, so maybe we should put it on the third small wagon. We probably should ask the young ones to gather whatever buffalo chips they can, and then throw them on the tarp under the second wagon."

Abigail took the seat on the first wagon. KaSandra took the seat on the second wagon with Brandy on the seat of the smaller third wagon. Reminton was bringing up the rear behind the third wagon, and there were two kids on each side of the second wagon picking up buffalo chips. The young ones would laugh every time one of the wagon wheels would bust a buffalo chip, and a click beetle would fly out and then land on its back.

Rusty would run from one beetle to the next, but he never tried to bite one. Rusty had been bitten on the hip sometime back, and he hadn't forgotten that it hurt. Shermon rode up and said, "We have made real good time. You guys sure gathered a lot of chips. Did you pick up chips the whole day?" Dakota said, "No uncle Sherm, there was so many, it didn't take no time to have the tarp full of buffalo chips." Shermon said, "Well there's some ducks flying up ahead, so I could use a couple of shooters." Dakota and Logan both agreed to go.

Shermon said, "Let's pull the wagons over close to that bluff, and under the cover of those trees. We will unhook the oxen from the wagons and water the Remuda." down at the water's edge, Reminton said, "This sick ox doesn't want any water." Shermon said, "We will just let him be. See that taurine all over the front of the ox? It is colorless, and it's a bile which is taurocholic acid. You see how its legs and feet are about double the size they should be? You wouldn't believe what's happening on its insides.

This is nice water, but the trees are hedge wood, which is a very hard, yellow wood and it's really not good burning wood." Shermon continued, "Reminton, do you want to get three of those 12 gauge side by sides, and shells? Also get me one of those 22 rifles and a handful of 22 shells." He said, "Lance, you and Wyatt don't mind if we four go shoot some ducks do ya?" Lance said, "No, go ahead, we will have a nice fire ready when you get back."

Lance and Wyatt brought over some Buffalo chips and gathered what deadwood there was. Then they replaced some large rocks that were already there. Dakota asked, "What's the 22 rifle for uncle Sherm? Shermon said, "Well, if we shoot a duck, and it goes down but it is not dead, we can shoot it in the head and then Rusty will bring it to us. Dakota and Logan loaded a 12-gauge."

Shermon said, "Try to lead them almost a foot when you shoot, they are flying fast". The first ducks flew over, and they shot three of them. Sure enough there was one sitting in the water. Shermon shot the duck in the head, and Rusty brought it in along with the other two. As four more ducks flew over they shot them and Rusty retrieved them. Shermon said, "Seven large ducks is plenty. Let's leave some for the next hunters." He continued, "That was fun, but I think Rusty had as much fun as we did." Dakota asked his dad Reminton why they did all the hunting, and uncle Lance and uncle Wyatt did not do any of the hunting? Reminton said, "Lance and Wyatt hunted some when they were younger, but never took a liking to it like Shermon and I did."

Shermon said, let's get back and maybe we will just de-breast the seven Ducks. Seven large duck breast is a lot of meat." So, back away from the camp they de-breasted the seven ducks, and had fourteen nice large half breasts. KaSandra suggested frying the fourteen half breasts in their own grease with some flour, salt, and pepper seed. Reminton said, "That sounds real good." So she fried the large half breast, and they made some biscuits, and cut thin sliced potatoes. Then they had black coffee and even some sun tea. Shermon raved over how good the meal was, and everyone else agreed.

We have a little time before sundown, so let me help clean up this mess. KaSandra would not hear of it. She said, "You guys have another cup of coffee and we will take care of this."

CHAPTER 26
THE ATTACK OF THE WOLVES

Reminton said, "We sure have a lot of buffalo chips left." Shermon said, "Well, let's build up the fire and we will pick up some more tomorrow. " Lance said, "That sick ox is up and moving away." KaSandra said, "Should we bring it back?" Shermon said, "No, let it leave. It's too far gone. I'm sure it is going off to die. Tomorrow we will hook the biggest ox to the small wagon, and then two to the other two wagons. That big ox won't have any trouble pulling that small wagon, but if he does, we can hook Rusty on there with him!" Then he laughed.

A little bit later Shermon said, "Don't get worried but I see a few braves moving out on those flats, but it's Apaches." Then Shermon spotted Geronimo with about thirty more braves. Shermon said, "Not to worry, but something isn't right." Shermon walked out into the open night and Reminton walked with him. Geronimo rode up with maybe ten braves and Geronimo put up his hand, and Shermon put up his in peace.

Geronimo spoke and said, "Shermon, my white warrior brother, there is much grief in our village." Shermon said, "What is it, and what can my family do to help?" Geronimo said, "Two nights ago wolves came into our village and slipped away with a small child. We killed five wolves but last night the wolves came back and slipped away with another small child. Our village is on twenty-four hour watch, but we have to have the heads of the wolves so our small ones can go to the happy hunting grounds."

Shermon said, "I understand Geronimo and if my family and me see the wolves, we will bring you their heads." Geronimo said, "Be safe Shermon. You know that normally wolves are sacred to the Indian, but these are renegades, and they must be killed!" Shermon said, "We will kill them for our brothers if we see them." Geronimo said, "Shermon, keep your family safe. These are very bad and dangerous wolves my white warrior brother."

Shermon said, "We will be safe, and we will keep our guard up." Geronimo said, "We will chase these wolves to the end of the Indian territory and back through the white man's territory until we have their heads on our lodge poles." Then Geronimo said to his braves, "Make a path a mile wide and we will run those wolves down!"

As the Apaches rode away, Shermon said, "Well I believe we had better watch for killer wolves. They run in a pack as many as ten, twelve, or even more sometimes." Shermon continued, "Lance, you, Reminton, and Wyatt each take a wagon, and put your wives and kids in the wagon. Close the back flaps on the bonnet and tie it shut. Then all you have to do is watch towards the front. Just stay awake and keep your guns ready."

KaSandra said, "What about you Sherm?" Shermon said, "I will be fine. I will crawl up in that large hedge wood and watch the wagons and the stock. Lance you and Reminton and Wyatt put your family behind you, and between you and the heavy back flaps of the bonnet, and together everyone will be safe. If a wolf comes in, it will be through the front and you will know it. A wolf can't help but growl and you will hear it."

Shermon noticed that Buck raised his head up and flared his nostrils. Shermon put his rifle to his shoulder. As Shermon watched however, there was a raccoon that scampered past and made very little noise. Shermon said, "Good boy Buck!"

The camp was waking up and Shermon said, "Well, I hope them Apaches killed those wolves, but until we know for sure, we will have to be double careful." Don't walk out of camp, or to the privy without a guard. I would like everyone to keep a gun handy at all times." Then Shermon sat on his heels and poured a cup of coffee. He said, "Everyone needs to be real careful. After we eat a biscuit, we will break camp, and then Lance, if you, Reminton and Wyatt want to, you can catch a couple hours of sleep."

Reminton said, "I am fine, but what about you?" Shermon said, "I will get enough sleep when I die." As they were breaking camp, Valerie said, "I need to use the privy. Wyatt and Brandy walked with her, while Valerie was in the privy and Rusty was at the "so called door."

Brandy and Wyatt were both looking towards the woods when Valerie started screaming for all she was worth. As they looked toward Valerie, they saw the biggest wolf they had ever seen, right at the privy! Rusty got between the wolf and Valerie, but the wolf was every bit as big as Rusty. Valerie took off running towards her mom and dad. Just as she was running, another large wolf stepped out of the trees and was in her path. It was behind her, making it difficult for Wyatt or Brandy too shoot.

Valerie screamed again, just as the wolf leaped from the ground to pounce on her. Dakota shot twice, and hit the wolf both times, but it still got back on its feet. By this time, Valerie had fallen to the ground, making it easy for Wyatt and Brandy to hit the wolf again.

Shermon yelled, "Lance, you and KaSandra watch the camp, "Then he and Reminton ran towards the privy. Katelyn screamed while running away from one wolf, she was running right into the path of another one that was growling and showing his teeth. Katelyn fell but luckily KaSandra was able to put two bullets in the wolf, as he sprang towards Katelyn.

The wolf just lay lifeless as he lay on top of Katelyn, and she couldn't stop screaming as she lay under the large wolf. Lance walked over to drag the large wolf off of Katelyn. He picked her up and told her she was ok, but she could not stop crying.

There were two wolves that had Rusty down, and Wyatt grabbed one by the scruff of his hair, and threw the wolf to the ground. As soon as the wolf hit the ground, he sprang back at Wyatt. Then Shermon and Reminton both put a bullet in the wolf and he fell dead. As Reminton turned around, another wolf sprung up at him. Reminton hit the wolf so hard that he broke his rifle. This didn't stop the wolf. As he came back at Reminton, he pulled his colt 44 and shot two bullets into the wolf's head.

There was another wolf circling KaSandra. As she was trying to put shells in her pistol, the wolf jumped for her. She fired twice and the wolf fell dead. Shermon noticed that two more wolves had Rusty down. He put his rifle to one of the wolves head and pulled the trigger, and the wolf fell dead. He tried to shoot the other wolf, but his guns were empty. As the wolf lunged for Shermon, he pulled his knife and they both fell into the trees. Both Reminton and Dakota wanted to shoot the wolf, but they were afraid they would hit Shermon.

As Shermon fell back, with the wolf snapping at his face, he held the wolf back with one hand, and with the other, he drove his bowie into the wolf's chest three times. Each time he stabbed the wolf, the wolf would cry out. Then after the struggle, the wolf lay dead. Reminton helped Shermon up and Shermon headed right over to where Rusty lay. Shermon said, "Rusty is in a bad way," as the whole family made their way to where Rusty lay. Rusty tried to lift his head when Valerie sat down next to him. Valerie cried, "My big dog. You saved me Rusty but why did you try to fight all those wolves?"

Valerie was shaking and crying real hard when Katelyn and Brandy sat down next to her. Wyatt said, "Rusty you are some dog," as he turned and walked away rubbing his eyes. Wyatt stood back where Reminton and Dakota were. Shermon walked up and said, 'I'm sure it's over, but we had better make sure we watch our backs.

As they quietly stood around, Rusty reached up and licked Valerie's face one more time as he closed his big eyes and took his last breath. Valerie laid her head on Rusty and cried herself to sleep. KaSandra, Abigail, and most everyone else were fighting back their tears.

Shermon and Reminton noticed five Apache braves standing close to their camp. Then Geronimo came up and was standing with maybe ten or twelve more braves. Geronimo, nor the braves made a sound, they just stood there. Shermon raised his hand and said, 'Our red brothers, our warrior dog is dead, but he did real good trying to protect us before the wolves took him down. There is six dead wolves. They came into our camp, and with Rusty's help, we killed them."

Geronimo said, "The dead wolves make me and my people happy, but we are sorry about your warrior dog." Shermon said, "Take the wolves and put their heads upon your lodge poles." Geronimo said, 'I see the sorrow in your eyes, the same as in our eyes. We have a warrior dog, with warrior pups. We will give you a warrior pup and he will grow large like your dead warrior dog." Then Geronimo raised his hand in peace, the same as Shermon. Then the Apaches left and took the wolves with them.

Shermon began making small talk, or conversation and everyone knew it, but what else was there? Reminton and Dakota was wiping down some guns and reloading them when Dakota said, "You know Sherm, that girl needs another dog." Reminton said, "Dakota, do you think she will take another dog?" Dakota said, "Probably not," and turned his head and sniffed as he walked away. He said, "Well there is probably not another dog out there that could take Rusty's place anyway."

Lance and Wyatt dug a hole as Wyatt said, "I'm going to miss that dog!" Reminton said, "We are all going to miss Rusty." Lance said, "It was like that dog belonged to all of us, anyway he acted like he was a McBay." Shermon said, "Well, Christmas is two weeks away and then maybe two more weeks to Waco!" Valerie was awake and crying softly and they heard her say, "Rusty, why, did you think that you had to take on all of those wolves by yourself?"

Brandy went and got the blanket that Rusty laid on in the wagon. She said, "Valerie, I got Rusty's favorite blanket from the wagon. With a lot of tears, KaSandra, Brandy, and Valerie wrapped the large blanket around Rusty, as Abigail and Katelyn helped. Shermon and Wyatt lifted the big dog and laid him in the shallow grave. Then everyone was telling Rusty how much they would miss him, as they placed rocks on his grave.

Shermon said to Valerie, 'Valerie, honey, you know how much Ma Mc-Bay loved Rusty, right?" Valerie said, "I know, and Rusty loved her too uncle Sherm. Don't you think Rusty is in heaven with Ma McBay now? I still miss Rusty.' Shermon said, "We all do and we will think about Rusty all of the time, but I can't help but think of how happy Ma McBay is right now with her own dog in heaven!"

While Shermon was talking with Valerie, KaSandra, Abigail, and Brandy were making plans to work on Shermon's buckskins that KaSandra had brought back from Edorado. KaSandra said, "Maybe we can ask Dakota and Logan to sit on the wagon seats while we work on Shermon's buckskins?"

Brandy said, "Yes, it will probably only take two or three days to cut and stitch the buckskin."

Shermon said, "Here comes Geronimo." Geronimo rode into camp with a couple of his braves. His one hand was up in peace, but in his other hand, he held a pup. He said, 'I have come with a warrior pup to replace your warrior dog.' Shermon said, "I will be right back," and walked over to the place where Valerie was sitting close to Rusty's grave.

Valerie said in a low voice where Geronimo could not hear her, "Uncle Sherm, I don't want another dog." Shermon said, "I know that you don't, but we can't refuse to take a gift from Geronimo. You don't have to keep the pup any longer than you want to." Valerie said, "I understand uncle Sherm. I will act like I want it, but I won't keep it."

Shermon said, "Thanks honey," and then Shermon and Valerie walked over to where Geronimo was. Geronimo said, "I brought you a pup, and he will become a warrior dog like the other one you had." Valerie took the pup and said, 'Thank you Mr. Geronimo. I will take good care of him, and some-day he will be a warrior dog."

Shermon thanked Geronimo, and Geronimo said, "Pup will be good war-rior dog someday." Shermon said, "I'm sure he will, and thank you again." Geronimo said, "Thank you and your family as well. The Apaches have all the wolves' heads on their lodge poles.' Then Geronimo raised his hand, and Shermon did the same, as he and the braves left.

Shermon walked by the wagon where Valerie and the pup were. He heard Valerie say, "Stay on the floor, you silly pup. I only took you because uncle Sherm asked me to." Shermon said, "Where's that silly pup with the blue eye? I need to find it and lead it out into the woods because who knows how big he will get." Valerie said, "Uncle Sherm, I have the pup in here. I thought maybe I should feed and water it some, then we could see how big it might get." Shermon said, "Well Valerie, if you want to try, then I think we should. As Shermon was walking away, he heard Valerie say, "Come here blue, so I can hold you." Then she said, "I'm only doing this because me and uncle Sherm wants to see how big you get!"

CHAPTER 27
THE GHOST DANCER

Shermon asked Valerie, "Do you think we should get back on the trail? You know, it's almost Christmas, and then only a couple more weeks and we will be in Waco." No one else said anything. Valerie said with tears rolling down her face, "Uncle Sherm, what about Rusty?" Shermon stepped right in and said, "Remember Valerie, Rusty is in heaven with Ma McBay now." Valerie said, "That's right uncle Sherm, I just forgot for a minute! I'm ready to put some miles behind us."

Brandy walked over and asked, "Are you ok now, honey?" Valerie said, "I will miss Rusty, but I know he is in heaven with Ma McBay now. Mom you know that Ma McBay loved Rusty, so she has a dog in heaven with her and it is Rusty! Plus, me and uncle Sherm want to see how big, Blue gets, and maybe someday he will be a warrior dog just like Rusty."

Shermon said, "Let's break camp. You heard Valerie, let's put some miles behind us." They made sure the fire was out, and took their places in the small wagon train. Shermon said, "The weather is beautiful," and they all agreed.

Shermon asked, Are we ready to put some miles behind us?" Remington said, "The camp is clean, and we left some dead wood by the fire pit for the next ones that are through here." Lance said, "We have the largest ox hooked to the third wagon, and it looks like he is ready." Sherm said, "I won't be far ahead," and then said, "See you in heaven Rusty but I hope not too soon." KaSandra told Katelyn that she could ride with Valerie and play with the pup. Katelyn asked Valerie, "What are you going to name that pup?" Valerie said, "Well, because he has one blue eye, I think I will name him Blue." Katelyn said, "I think that name is right."

Later, Shermon dropped back a little and asked Reminton, "Why do you think that Lance is driving one wagon, and Logan the second, and then Dakota driving the third wagon?" Remington said, "Well big brother, you are the one that keeps saying Christmas Is almost here. So I would say it probably has something to do with Christmas." Shermon said, I guess that makes sense." Shermon did not have any idea that what the women were working on was for him. He just figured it was for the four young ones and said, "That was good."

Shermon was sitting on Buck, waiting for the small wagon train. Reminton asked, "What's up Sherm?" Shermon said, "The Apaches have fires on four sides and I don't think that we should pull through their fires." While Shermon was saying it, he thought it might also be disrespectful. Then Geronimo with maybe fifteen braves rode up. They all put their hand up in peace. Shermon asked, "What is all the fires for?" Geronimo replied, "We are getting ready for the Ghost Dance. The Ghost Dance will last all through the night. The dance is to honor the two small children and your big Warrior dog. It also will disgrace the wolves for what they have done. We would like for you and your family to stay and join us for the Ghost Dance." Shermon said, "Let me talk to my family, and then we will stay." Shermon continued, "I'm sure that we made at least ten miles today, and I think we should stay for the Ghost Dance. I believe it would be good for the Apaches and us if we all stayed for the Ghost Dance.

The McBays pulled over and unhooked the oxen and then picketed their Remuda. Shermon said, "I don't think we should put up our dinner tarp, I think it will be good under the stars. It looks like a beautiful night." He continued, "I thought we were off to one side, but instead it looks like we are in the middle, and it also looks like it was planned by Geronimo. Let's start a fire and put on some coffee."

The McBays were building a fire, when Geronimo walked up and said, "Make all the fires you want to, but the Apaches will supply the meal." The

Apaches had quite a few fires going, but they had a large buffalo on one fire, and two large deer on two other fires. Reminton looked at all the ears of corn roasting in the fires. KaSandra said, "It looks like they have a wagon load of large potatoes roasting also." Brandy said, "Look at those large pots of beans!" Dakota said, "Something sure smells good." Shermon said, "One of the things you smell, that smells so good is the sassafras tea that they are boiling." KaSandra asked Shermon, "Would you want to drink their tea,or the hot black coffee on our fire?" Shermon said, "I will drink the coffee."

The Indians kept bringing food to the McBays, when Shermon finally said, "We can eat no more!" Geronimo was smoking a peace pipe with a couple of his higher ranked braves. He asked Shermon if he and his brothers would like to join them. Shermon, Lance, and Reminton sat down with Geronimo, but Wyatt said to Shermon, "You know I would rather not smoke anything," then he asked Shermon if he thought Geronimo would understand if he did not smoke with them. Shermon said, "I am sure it will be ok." Then the drums started and Wyatt told Shermon, "Tell Geronimo I will dance with his braves, if it's ok?" Shermon talked to Geronimo, and Geronimo felt it would be good if the "big" man danced with his braves.

Wyatt was not near as tall as Shermon or his other two brothers, but he made it up in his size. Like Shermon said when he got back home, "Wyatt, I can hardly believe how big your arms and chest are. Are you as strong as you look?" Reminton said, "Shermon, Wyatt is as strong as he looks." Then Shermon saw how strong Wyatt was when Wyatt picked him up and held him over his head. Shermon said, "You can put me down. You are very strong!"

The next morning Shermon said to the family, "That was some dance!" Wyatt if you weren't so big, at times out there, I thought you looked just like one of Geronimo's braves." Lance said, "I can't believe how the whole tribe left so quietly. They were up all night dancing and eating and then leave without sleep?" Shermon said, "Geronimo's braves rotate sleep the same as we do on night guard. When they are on the move, they take turns sleeping." Then he said, "Have you seen all the gifts the Apaches left?" The McBays could not believe all of the jewelry, blankets and other items that the Apaches left for the family.

KaSandra said, "We should have given the Apaches something." Shermon said, "When the Apaches are given anything, they feel they have to give back something better or they will lose fate. So anyway KaSandra, the final outcome is that the Indians have to be better givers. So there is probably a lot of white people who could learn from the Indians. It is better to give than to receive.

CHAPTER 28
CHRISTMAS

The McBays hooked up the oxen, filled the water barrels, and tied the quarter horses to their wagons. Shermon watched his two brothers; Lance and Wyatt both take a wagon seat with Dakota and Logan driving the third wagon. Reminton was on drag, pulling up the rear.

Later that day, Shermon watched the women retake the wagon seats, and the men mount their horses, so he said to Reminton, "I guess the women got done with whatever they were making for the young ones." Reminton said, "I guess so," and did not say anymore. Shermon said, "Well I guess it's none too soon because Christmas is tomorrow. Let's try for two more miles. There is good water and tall grass up ahead, with a real nice bluff that we can camp at. You can see for miles from it! I know there are pheasants in the tall grass, and pheasant would be great for our Christmas meal." Reminton said, "Sounds good to me." Shermon said, "Pass the word, two more miles and we will make camp. Also tell them about the pheasants. That will give them something else to think about."

Right about two miles up, Reminton said, "Shermon is waving us to the right." So the small wagon train pulled up to the spot where Shermon had picked. KaSandra said, "This is a real beautiful place!" Shermon said, "Dakota, you and Logan make sure you picket the Remuda where they can't reach the water." Logan asked, "Why don't we leave them at the water's edge? Do you think they would cross the water?" Shermon said, "No, the reason we picket them after they drink is because if we didn't they would founder."

Logan asked, "What do you mean uncle Sherm?" Shermon said, "Wild horses would not, but a horse in a Remuda would fill up on water, and it could kill them if they drank too much. The same goes for most any animal on a rope. They would stay and keep drinking. That's why we always picket them in a nice grassy area, and away from the water."

KaSandra said, "Shermon, there is coffee ready. Do you want me to get you a cup?" Shermon said, "I will get it. But thanks anyway." Then he said, "How about fish tonight and pheasant tomorrow?" That's all it took. Dakota was digging out the fishing poles.The girls were playing with Blue when Valerie said, "Blue will never be Rusty." She knew that Rusty was with Ma McBay, and she knew that Rusty would want Valerie to have Blue while he was with Ma.

The Boys had already caught five fish, so KaSandra said, "Looks like fish for dinner!" They melted some lard/fat and sliced some potatoes real thin for fried chips. Before the lard/fat had turned to grease, Shermon and the boys had already caught fourteen nice fish and were cleaning them. The fourteen fish were large rainbow trout that they left whole.

The McBays had rainbow trout, fried potato chips, biscuits, black coffee and sassafras roots that they made sun tea with. The Indians had given the McBays, potatoes, corn and sassafras roots, and the sassafras roots were a big hit, especially with the young ones. Shermon said, "We need to bury those fish bones so that pup, Blue, can't get to them." KaSandra said, "Shermon while you were smoking with Geronimo, us women were busy!" Shermon asked, "What were you women busy doing?"

Brandy said, "We were stitching up shoulder straps for the braves, and they liked them so much that I think that is why they gave us so much food!" Shermon said, "You are probably right, and I am glad they had the food to give us! Tomorrow morning, I think I will walk over in that tall grass and see if I can kick up a couple of pheasants. Anybody else want to go?"

Dakota and Logan both said, "I will go!" Shermon said, "Well, why don't you two get three 12 gauge side by sides, and a box of 12 gauge shells and put them in the third wagon. I would like to leave early, hopefully by sun up.

Shermon then asked his brothers, "Do you care if me and these young men have some fun and shoot a couple pheasants in the morning?" Reminton said, "I will make sure they are up and ready." Dakota said, "We will be ready! We will sleep out here tonight!"

Shermon said, "Well, let's set up night guard." Reminton said, "We have night guard already set up Sherm, and we will see you in the morning." Shermon said, "Reminton, are you ready to take over this family?" Reminton said, "Shermon you are in charge but we would like to give you the night off if you would let us? Let's say it's because tomorrow is Christmas." Shermon smiled a little and said, "Ok, you three have the night guard, but wake me if you need to."

Shermon poured the rest of his coffee in the fire, then walked over to Buck and said something. He then crawled in his bed roll, rolled over and fell to sleep, with Buck standing close to him. Reminton said, "Well I think Shermon is really starting to believe in us." Lance said, "Yes, he would not have crawled into his bed roll like that a month ago." Wyatt said "I don't think he would have even a week ago." Reminton said, "We all know that Shermon believes in us but look at Buck. Shermon also knows Buck is on night guard with us." Wyatt said, "What do you think Shermon said to Buck before he rolled in?" Reminton said, "Shermon probably said, I'm sure they will be okay, but wake me if you need to!"

Shermon's three younger brothers took turns at night watch, and they were proud that Shermon respected them enough to crawl into his bed roll and let them have night watch. Reminton was sitting on a long tree stump by the fire, when Shermon crawled out of his bed roll. Reminton shifted over a little so Shermon would have room to sit down, and asked, "How did you sleep big brother?" Shermon said, "I don't know when I have slept any better than last night."

Reminton said, "I know you also had Buck on night guard, and I was wondering what you said to him. Shermon said, "I told Buck to get some sleep, and that my brothers had night guard covered. Shermon smiled and said, Reminton, you Lance, and Wyatt plus the rest of our family, have earned my trust and respect.

I could not be any prouder of you all." Reminton said, "Sherm, I am talking for all of us because we have all talked." He continued, "Sherm, none of us had any idea that you are the man that you are. We knew that you were good, but you are better than just good. We all know how lucky we are to have you as a brother. I am not trying to get sentimental, but we all love you very much." Shermon said, "Reminton, I know that we don't say it often and maybe we should say it more, but I love all of you." He then said, as he was clearing his throat, "The sun is coming up, so I guess I had better shake those two out of their bed rolls. Dakota and Logan walked up with the three 12 gauge side by sides, and Dakota asked, "Well, did you change your mind, or are we going hunting?" Shermon asked, "Do you have the shells?" Dakota said, "Me and Logan both have a pocket full of shells."

Shermon said, "Well hand me one of those guns, and a couple shells and let's go." As Shermon and the two young men walked out of camp, Reminton said to himself, "There goes a hell of a man." Reminton was at the fire, pouring himself another cup of coffee, when KaSandra walked up and asked, "Have the hunters left already?" Reminton said, "Yeah they just made it to the tall grass," and before Remington or KaSandra could say anything else, there were shotguns going off.

KaSandra said, "Well, I guess we should get some water on the fire to boil, but first look at these buckskins we made for Sherman." Reminton said, "Those are great!" Lance and Wyatt both walked up and said, "They sure are." KaSandra said, "So, you think he will like them?" All three brothers said, "You bet he will. Then there were three more shots fired. Reminton said, "Well you'd better hide them buckskins, because I see Shermon, Dakota and Logan already heading back this way.

They put on some water to boil, and Reminton said, "This morning I told Shermon how proud and grateful we were to be a part of his family, but he turned it around and said he could not be more proud of us, and how lucky he was to be in our family. Shermon was carrying the three side by sides, and Dakota had two birds and Logan had two birds. Reminton said, "Those sure are four nice looking cock pheasants, but why is Shermon carrying all three of the guns?" Dakota and Logan looked at each other. Shermon said "Well, they each shot two birds and I said, you guys got the birds, so I will carry the guns back while you two carry the birds that you shot!"

Dakota said, "That's right, uncle Sherm gave us the first shot on all four birds, and a second shot was not needed. Shermon said, "Yeah you two did real good, but now you both get to help me clean these four pheasants." Dakota and Logan both said they were ready. Shermon said, "Let's get these birds in that hot water so we can remove their feathers."

KaSandra said, "How about we cut those birds into six pieces each, and fry them in flour and pepper seed?" Reminton said, "That sounds real good, but how about some onions fried with the birds?" Shermon said, "And maybe a biscuit or two plus some of that corn that the Apaches gave us."

KaSandra said, "Hey big man, I thought you were worried about getting fat?" Shermon said, "Well, it is Christmas, right?" KaSandra said, "Yes, it is Christmas!" Brandy said, "We could leave the husks on the corn and put it right in the coals of the fire." Abigail said, "I will start some sassafras tea." When everything was ready, KaSandra asked, "Can we hold hands and pray first?" KaSandra prayed and the rest of the family joined in.

"The Lord bless us,

The Lord, make His face to shine on us, and be gracious to us,

The Lord, look upon us with favor and give us peace."

Then KaSandra added, "And thank you for this meal, and for our family Lord. They all said, "In Jesus name, Amen."

After they had all finished eating, Shermon said, "Well that was one of the best meals I've ever had, I do believe!" Valerie said, "Uncle Shermon, you always say that!" Shermon said, "Maybe I do, but that was a great meal." KaSandra said, "Do you all want to sing a couple of Christmas songs?" There were some good voices in the McBay family! KaSandra started the McBays in Joy to the World and Silent night, plus a couple of other songs in which they all sang.

Shermon said, "It looks like everyone has either coffee or sassafras tea to drink." He then asked the four young ones to come over to see what he had for them. He pulled out two perfectly carved dolls that he had carved and had hidden in his saddle bags for the girls.

Both Katelyn and Valerie squealed a little and hugged Shermon as he handed the two dolls to them. Then Shermon handed Dakota, and Logan each a slingshot that he had made for them and asked them if they thought they could get enough pebbles to shoot?

Dakota and Logan were both so happy with the two slingshots, that when Shermon reached out to shake their hands, they both hugged him real tight! Blue was sitting there by him and Shermon reached in his saddlebag and handed blue a block of wood, and Blue started chewing on it.

After the excitement of the gifts settled in, the four children told Shermon that they had something for him too. Shermon said, "For me? I don't think that I need anything." All four kids said at once, "We bet you will want this," and they handed Shermon a large, brown paper wrapped present. Shermon said, "Now, what could this be?"

Dakota said, "Open it uncle Sherm!" So Shermon tore open the package and not only was he surprised, but he was also speechless for a moment. Shermon finally said, "Now this is the best looking buckskin shirt and pair of buckskin trousers that I have ever seen!"

KaSandra said, "Try them on Sherm and if we need to alter them, we can." Shermon tried them on and said, "Look, this shirt and these trousers look like they were made just for me!" All of the other McBays said they thought they were also. Sherm said, "How did you make them, and where did you get the material? They fit me perfect, I would say!" And they all agreed.

KaSandra said, "When I went to Edorado with you and Reminton, I got the buckskin at the general store. I bought all they had, and it was good that I did. Then Abigail, Brandy and me, made the buckskin shirt and trousers in the back of the wagon so you would not see them." Shermon said, "Well, you really surprised me! I know how much work goes in to making buckskin clothes, and I can't thank you all enough." KaSandra said, "Sherm, you already thanked us more than you might know. We wanted to show you how much we appreciate all you've done for us. I would like to sing one more song."

KaSandra sang, "Oh Come All Ye Faithful," and the rest of the McBays enjoyed the song and her voice by just listening. Then KaSandra said, "Before you set up night camp, I would like to say a prayer," and all he McBays joined in.

They prayed:

As I lay me down to sleep,

I pray the Lord my soul to keep,

If I die before I wake,

I pray the Lord my soul to take, amen.

Lance said he would take the first night guard. The women split up in the two large wagons, with Blue and Valerie in the first wagon. Shermon said, "We will split up under the first and second wagon." Reminton said, "I will relieve Lance in a couple of hours. Then Wyatt, if you want, you can relieve me." When Wyatt relieved Reminton, Wyatt said, "I noticed that Shermon was up. I guess he just couldn't sleep." So, on his way to get a couple more hours of sleep, Reminton asked Shermon, "Aren't you tired, big brother?"

Shermon said, "I've had four good hours of sleep and I am wide awake. I might be a little anxious about getting to Waco. You know we could be on our lands in about two weeks?" Reminton said, "We did good big brother, but unless you want company at this fire, I am going to grab a couple more hours of sleep. " Shermon said, "You go ahead. I will see you in the morning about sun up."

In the morning, they had biscuits and gravy, and smoked bacon, with hot black coffee, and Shermon said, "That was a great meal!" Then he said, "It looks like it's going to be a beautiful morning.

CHAPTER 29
THE MCBAYS ADD ANOTHER PERSON TO THE WAGON TRAIN

As the McBays finished breakfast, Shermon said, "I believe we will be in Waco, on our land in two weeks." KaSandra said, "I know we are all very excited. Even with the wolves and Navajos, and the tornado, we sure have had some great times on this trail." Shermon added, "And some real good meals!" KaSandra said, "Shermon, when we get to our land, we will have good meals, and maybe even better ones!" Shermon said, "Well then, this is the beginning. My plans include us all growing old together. Let's clean up camp, and put some miles behind us." They closed up camp and hooked the oxen to the wagons. The women took the wagon seats and Valerie put Blue in the wagon and noticed that he was getting bigger.

Dakota and Logan rode close enough where they could talk, but they knew to also watch the trail. Reminton was pulling point, while Shermon was up ahead. Reminton yelled, "Lance, you hear that gun fire up ahead?" Lance said that he heard it then asked, "What do you think Rem?"

Reminton said, "Let's hold our ground," and then said, "Look over there, across the front of us." As they had discussed, Reminton moved up ahead a little and Wyatt dropped back to cover the drag. Then Shermon yelled and took off. He had seen three Navajo's chasing a young girl. Shermon had his rifle ready. He fired and knocked the first Navajo off his horse. The girl saw Shermon, and Shermon yelled for her to come his way. Shermon fired again and sent the second Navajo off of his horse, and the third Navajo headed for cover. Shermon pulled up to the young girl. As he was watching the tree line, he was praying that his family would not be under attack again.

The girl told Shermon that the Indians had her dad pinned down up ahead and she knew he had been shot at least once and maybe twice. Shermon said, "I will try to help your dad. Go the way that I have just come and my family is over there. Stay with them and I will do what I can."

With all the shooting, Reminton had the women to pull the wagons in a triangle. They were all praying, "Not another attack!" There were a couple more shots, and then a couple more. Shermon said again, "Ride over to my family and I will see about your dad."

The girl headed out towards where Shermon had come from. Then she saw the small wagon train. KaSandra said, "There is a girl out there!" Reminton was still on his horse and said, "I will be right back." Reminton yelled and kicked his horse and then headed to the girl. There was a Navajo that had made it around Shermon and was getting close. Kasandra shot the Indian and yelled at Reminton to bring the girl.

Shermon had kicked Buck into gear and was headed to help the girls' dad. Valerie and Katelyn were crying and Wyatt said, "Don't worry girls, we will be ok." Valerie said, "We are going to be attacked again!" Reminton said, "There is a lot of shooting where Shermon went."

The girl spoke and said, "A big man told me to come this way. Some Indians have my dad pinned down." Dakota said, "I see two Indians heading across over there." He then asked his dad, "Do you think we should go and help uncle Sherm?" They heard three more shots, then two more, and then they heard one single shot almost five minutes later.

Wyatt said, "Dakota, I know that you are worried about uncle Sherm the same as we are, but we need to wait and just hope everything is ok. We can't leave our small wagon train." Logan and the two girls were looking at the girl that Reminton had brought back to camp. Dakota walked up and asked the girl, "What is your name?" The girl said, "Lexi Lee, what's yours?"

Dakota said, "Dakota McBay," and added, "My uncle Sherm will help your dad if he can, but for now, you are safe with us." Lexi said, "Well Dakota McBay, I hope your uncle can help my dad but it did not look good."

About that time, they saw Shermon riding back towards them and he had another horse with him, but there was no rider. They all looked at Lexi. As Shermon rode up, Lexi asked Shermon where her dad was. Shermon said, "Your dad did not make it, but he went out fighting. He took a lot of the Navajos with him. Your dad was no quitter. He told me your name was Lexi Lee, and asked me if I would take you with us to Waco. I told your dad that we would take you with us. When I got to your dad, he was already in a bad way. He was hanging on and praying that you were safe. Your dad asked me to give you his horse, colt 44 and rifle, and his saddle bags. He said his skinning knife plus his live savings was in his saddle bags."

Lexi held back her tears and said, "Thank you Mr. McBay. I'm glad that you were with my dad when he died and that he was not alone." Shermon then said, "Well, now that there are no more Indians to shoot, I think we should go ahead and make camp. I was looking at a good place over there by that large oak tree. There is water and a small knoll that we can camp on and see for a long way.

Lexi said, "Did you bury my dad?" Shermon said, "Yes I did, after I shot the last four Indians. I sat with your dad until his time came. Then I dug a shallow grave and covered the grave with rocks." Lexi said, "Thank you again Mr. McBay." Shermon said, "You can call me Shermon if you'd like." Shermon said, "Let's make camp. Everyone needs to be careful, but I don't think there are any more Indians to worry about. The Indians that got Lexi's dad were just a few that left the reservation, renegades, I figure."

Lexi said, "I'm glad that they won't be going back to the reservation, or anywhere else." Shermon said, "Let's water the horses and unhook and water the oxen, then picket the horses under that large oak tree where the grass is good." Shermon said after the coffee was ready, that some coffee and a biscuit was all he needed. But on his plate, KaSandra had put some beans and smoked bacon with two biscuits.

When Shermon and Reminton were mostly to themselves, Reminton asked Shermon if Lexi's dad was dead when he reached him. Shermon said,

"No, but he was wishing he was dead!" Shermon said they had shot him four or five times and was scalping him when he rode up and shot the last three Indians. Shermon said, "It was hard for him to talk, but he was begging for me to shoot him."

Reminton then asked, "Did you Sherm?" Shermon said, "No. I handed him my gun and he put it to his head and pulled the trigger."

CHAPTER 30
THE MCBAYS AND LEXI ARRIVE IN WACO, TEXAS

Lexi slept right through the night, and right up until almost breakfast time. Shermon was sitting on his heels, pouring himself a cup of coffee. Lexi walked up and said, "Good morning Mr. McBay." Shermon said, "Lexi, you can call me Shermon, or Sherm if you'd like, because you've earned it." Lexi said, "Ok Sherm. Can I buy some biscuits and bacon from you? Then I will be on my way I guess."

Shermon said, "There's no price on food, and where would you go if you left us?" Lexi said, "I'm not sure where I'd go, Waco, I guess, but also I am not looking for a handout." Shermon said, "Lexi, I am not offering you a handout, you will earn what you get." Shermon then said, "We would like for you to stay with us and become part of the ranch we will build.

Lexi said, "Well I guess I can try it." "Ok, good. Do you drink coffee?" Lexi said, "I sure do." So Lexi took a tin cup and tried to sit on her heels like Shermon. Lexi poured herself a cup of coffee, and when she tasted it, she burnt her lip and could not believe how bad it tasted. Shermon said, "If you keep drinking it, someday you will like how it tastes."

After breakfast, Shermon said, "Well, that was a great meal," and he noticed that Lexi was drinking hot tea in her tin cup. He said, "The tea is good also." Then Lexi said, "They came up on us so quick. The Indians I mean. Luckily there was a small shelf that my dad and I was under. My dad had me behind him. I guess that's why I didn't get shot. We were under there for maybe a day and a half before the Indians got close and shot my dad in the shoulder, and then in his right leg.

My dad was begging me to get on Blackie and ride out while I still had a chance. My horse, Blackie, was tied to a tree behind where we were, when my dad said it was our only chance for me to ride out for help. But as soon as I lit out, I saw the Indians moving in on my dad, and I knew my dad was only wanting me to escape. I was riding Blackie for all he was worth, with two Indians on my heels and another one close by. That's when Shermon rode up and shot the two right behind me, and the other one headed the other way back towards my dad. Shermon saved me, and tried to save my Pa."

KaSandra then said, "Lexi, we are all so sorry about your dad, but we have talked, and we all want you to stay with us in Waco." Lexi agreed she would but asked, "Why Waco?" Dakota said, "Lexi, we have land in Waco, and we are going to build a large horse ranch."

Shermon said, "Lexi, there will be plenty of room, and plenty of things to do for everyone. If you decide to stay on, you would share a part of the ranch as your own." Reminton asked, "How many more miles do you think Shermon?" Shermon said, "I believe maybe fifty more miles until we reach Waco, and then our land is just on the other side of town. Let's get some shut eye. We have spent the day here, and we have rested some today. Tomorrow is Monday, so we will see about putting some miles behind us."

The three women, and the three girls, took wagon one, and two with Blue in the wagon with Valerie. The men and boys rolled their bed rolls out under the two wagons, except Lance and Logan, who took the first night watch. The night went without a hitch. It was a cool night without clouds, but with a lot of stars.

The next morning Shermon said to Buck his horse, "Well Buck, I believe it's going to be a beautiful day because it sure is a beautiful morning." He then walked over to the fire and said, good morning to KaSandra and Lexi who was raking the coals, and adding fuel to the fire. KaSandra poured Shermon a cup of coffee and then filled the large pot with more water, and added more coffee grounds. Shermon asked Lexi, "How did you sleep?" Lexi replied," I slept real good, how about you, Sherm?" Shermon said he slept good, also.

Reminton said a little later to Shermon, "I have noticed you are watching our back trail? Anything wrong Sherm?" Shermon said, "I don't believe so, but I did see a couple of Navajo braves on the prairie this morning, but it looked like they kept heading the way we came from." He continued, "I'm sure they did, but we need to be careful anyway."

After a good breakfast, they cleaned up camp. Shermon said, "Every day we get a little closer to our land, and a little farther out of Indian country. Let's hook up the oxen and bring the Remuda to the wagons, and put some miles behind us."

Everything was going well, and you could not have asked for better weather, when Shermon noticed a couple of men coming their way. Shermon dropped back a little and Reminton was sitting next to him when they realized that the two riders coming their way, was Wes Montana and Harry Austin.

Shermon asked them, "What brings you two out here? No trouble I hope?" Wes said, "No Sherm, but we knew you were getting close, so Cheyenne asked if we would ride out and meet you." Shermon said, "Well that's good, we are glad to have you."

Wes said, "Well if it's ok, I will stay up here on point." Harry Said, "Reminton, I will drop back a little with you, if it's ok?" Reminton said, "Sure, but let me tell my family that everything is ok." Shermon asked, "How's everything in Waco?" Wes said, "If you mean Cheyenne, she is doing good, but I know she is a little anxious for you to get to Waco." Shermon asked, "Do you really think so?" Wes said, "I know she is." Shermon said, "Good," and then he started Buck going a little faster.

That evening Shermon said, "Let's make camp at that river. It's called Red River." Wes said, "Sherm there is some catfish in that river that could even pull you in, I bet." Shermon said, "That would take a really big fish! It has been a couple of weeks or more since we had fish, and then he asked Dakota and Logan if they wanted to catch some fish for supper.

Lexi asked, "Hey Sherm, don't us girls get to fish if we want, or do the boys only get to fish?" Shermon said, "Anybody can fish that wants to." Lexi asked Katelyn and Valerie if they wanted to, but they both said, "No Lexi, but you go ahead if you want." So Lexi said, "I will go with you Dakota, and if I can, I will catch the biggest fish!" Dakota said, "You can try Lexi, but I don't think you will catch the biggest fish." Reminton said, "A little competition is good. " Dakota said, "Lexi, do you want me to get your pole ready?" Lexi said, "I think I had better get it myself, Dakota."

Reminton and Harry walked down to the river with Dakota, Logan and Lexi. Harry said, "This water is pretty swift, so be careful. Don't fall in, because you'd be in Waco before we could get you out I bet!" Shermon said, "How about a cup of coffee kid"

Shermon said, "It looks like they are catching something big." Wes said, "Let's walk down and see." Lexi had a monster fish on her line, but it had gotten wrapped up in Dakota's line. So between the two of them, they brought in a channel catfish that must have weighed more than twenty pounds. They said it was a tie because they both caught the biggest fish!

While they were cleaning the fish, Wes asked Shermon what his plans were when they reached Waco and their land. Shermon said, "First we will build some shelter, maybe a ranch house with plenty of room, and then probably a good sized bunkhouse. Shermon said, "I think the living quarters should be first. Then we will have a blacksmith shop, with inside and outside horse stalls. We will also have a gun room, where we can have gun repairs, and plenty of guns and ammo. There is some land adjoining ours that we will purchase later."

Wes Montana said, "Shermon, it sounds like you have given this a lot of thought." Shermon said, "Yes, I have. I am going to build a very large horse ranch, but I will need good people to help." Shermon continued, "Do you know some good people that would be interested?" Wes said, "I believe I do." Shermon said, "Good, but before I do any of this, I will look up Cheyenne." About that time KaSandra said, "Come and get it. Dinner is ready."

They had fried catfish, thin sliced potatoes, biscuits, hot black coffee and sassafras tea, which was a great hit! The meal was great and the weather was real good also. Shermon was talking more about Waco, and the plans he had for him and his family when they got there. As they sat around the fire, they talked to Wes and Harry about their Ma.

Lance and Harry took the first watch and Abigail brought them some coffee before turning in. It wasn't long before Reminton and Wyatt relieved Lance and Harry. Shermon and Wes took the third and final watch until sun up.

Shermon said, "Wes, look at that beautiful sunrise!" Wes Montana said, "Shermon there is going to be a lot more beautiful sunrises for you and your family when you reach Waco." As Shermon and Wes walked up to the coffee pot, Shermon said, "I have been watching ducks fly in and out of those cat-tails. What do you say we get some duck eggs for breakfast?"

Shermon, Reminton, and Wes walked over to the cattails and started gath-ering eggs. After a very short time, Shermon said, "I think we have plenty, let's leave the rest." As they walked back into camp, Shermon said as he counted the duck eggs, "I think we have thirty duck eggs."

KaSandra said, "Let's start frying them. The fire is ready and we have smoked bacon and biscuits, plus plenty of coffee." As they were eating, Sher-mon said, "This will be our last meal on the trail because we will be in Waco later today!"

Wes Montana and Harry Austin both agreed that they had never eaten as good as they had with the McBays on the trail. KaSandra said, "Shermon, it's a good thing we are close to Waco because we used the last of the flour. We are out of beans, smoked bacon, and we are very low on coffee!" Shermon said, "Well, let's get ready to roll! We don't want to run out of coffee," and he laughed.

Shermon said, "Let's hook up the oxen, and tie whatever horses we don't ride to the first and second wagon. The women took seats on the three wag-ons, and the girls were in the second wagon, playing with Blue. Shermon, Reminton, Lance, Wyatt, Dakota, Logan and Wes and Harry, all eight, rode in front of the wagons, with all three wagons rolling side by side with ten to twelve feet between them.

KaSandra was in the first wagon when Abigail and Brandy pulled up along the two sides. Brandy was on one side and Abigail was on the other side. Shermon's chest was sticking way out there with him and the seven other riders in front of the three wagons pulling side by side.

It was something to see, but the first thing they saw as they pulled through town was Cheyenne, sitting on a fifteen and a half hands tall chestnut horse, with four white socks and a large white diamond on his forehead. The horse was beautiful to look at, but not as beautiful to look at as Cheyenne.

Shermon smiled from ear to ear and said, "This is Cheyenne Decker, and Cheyenne, this is my family!"

THE END